FLIGHT

OF THE

RAVENHAWK

By J. Edward Hackett

Ink Smith Publishing

www.ink-smith.com

Printed in the U.S.A

The final approval for this literary material is granted by the author.

All characters appearing in this work are fictitious. Any resemblance to real persons, living or dead, is purely coincidental.

ISBN: 978-1-947578-34-0

Ink Smith Publishing
P.O. Box 361
Lakehurst, NJ 08733

For Ashley, the wife of my dreams and the only woman I know whose heart shines as brilliantly as the stars themselves.

"But you must not change one thing, one pebble, one grain of sand, until you know what good and evil follow on the act. The world is in balance, in Equilibrium. A wizard's power of Changing and of Summoning can shake the balance of the world. It is dangerous, that power. It is perilous. It must follow knowledge and serve need. To light a candle is to cast a shadow..."

~ The Master Changer to Ged in Ursula K. Le Guin's A Wizard of Earthsea

Before the Light, before Queen's book and scepter's might.
We hold these promises dear in our fight.
Each here will sincerely seek Darnashi's end;
For this we live, with all purposes amend.
To not do as yee will promise on this night shall lead to death's invite.
Let those who support Darnashi's life, know our strife.
As long as he lives, the three races will unite.
One front for one death, one treaty to draw last breath.
On this I swear!

~ The Sylvaran spelloath spoken at the War Council of the Three Races.

Prologue

Dorn slammed on the knocker. "My Lord! Wake!"

Kalero yawned, stirring in his heavy sleep. "What is it?" he called. The Wizardrium's armor clang in unison with heavy footfalls.

Dorn screamed, "Inspectors and Wizardslayers. They're inspecting the warehouse!"

Kalero jumped out of bed. After finding himself fatigued from one of the underground meetings in the catacombs over the guild warehouse and the printing press workshop, Kalero napped. His tunic and cloak already about him, he flicked his hand and satchel and staff floated to him in haste.

In seconds, Kalero ran alongside Dorn. His legs felt like weights; his body not even awake to the strenuous activity. They weaved and bobbed through a series of underground sewers and catacombs of the old city. Feet splattered puddles of muck and grime. Dorn's muscular back remained backlit from an outstretched torch, a dark silhouette leading Kalero to an uncertain fate. Flickers of flame danced shadows as nervously as the pitch in his voice when he had first awoken Prince Kalero.

"Where are we going?" Kal asked.

Without looking behind him or stopping, Dorn said, "My home. I built an access way after finding some passages of the Lower City. Venda stands now about eight feet higher than when it was first built."

"I think I am going to be sick. They're definitely near."

Throbbing entered, Kalero's skull. Atop the street, a small unit of enchanted armor with the alloy of the Wizardslayers could be felt stomping in unison. The presence of that armor and its alloy—Hecatium— radiated a field that drained magick from mageborne. He could feel his power waning; his head pounding matched the commotion from the troops above.

"Quickly!" Dorn shouted.

The Hecatium's field of influence lessened, and a sense of the world's enchantment returned. The pounding in his head ceased. The drain on his muscles regained some vigor. Hecatium drained the very lifeforce of a mageborne's soul, and if exposed long enough to the metal, then a mage would die.

Flight of the Ravenhawk

Since the tunnels wound in no predictable linear fashion, both Dorn and Kal snaked underneath the movements of the Wizardslayers above. Kal would enter various fields generated by the Hecatium armor, and then he would fall back. Dorn's strong arms would pull him. In minutes, however, they were beyond the immanent danger. Still, Kal dare not cast any magick. The troops above might well have a tracker, and if they were going to Dorn's home, Kal would not risk his family. Dorn had already risked much. Winding through passages, the damp walls muffled the sounds from above, and soon heavy footfalls faded only to be replaced by the sounds of running water and the scattering of rats. His sweat met the cold air, and Kalero shivered. For about three hours, he felt the coldness and refuse afoot.

Eventually, they came to wooden ladder bolted to the ceiling. Both held their knees panting. Hunched over, Dorn motioned for Kal to wait as he climbed up first. From his pocket, Dorn pulled a key that unlocked the door, and he motioned to a grated mat for Kal to wipe his feet. Dorn scraped his boots before climbing to the top. Then, he pushed open the hinged part, and a low light cascaded down into the passageway. Kal sighed heavily at the light above. Looking over his shoulder, he glanced worriedly back in the direction of the Wizardslayers. He worried about the pamphlets the Inspectors and the Wizardslayers would find. As the capital in the Allurian Empire, Venda was no longer a place of toleration and peace, and arguing for equality academically was no longer an academic exercise.

****

The Printing Press Guild Hall's door hung off its hinges. Wizardslayers hauled pamphlets and manuscripts out of the building and threw them into wagons outside. Several Wizardslayers held the print manager. He was cuffed in the office, and minutes later, he screamed from interrogation. Chardon could hear the delightful screams. Eventually, the man would sign the forced confession.

On the wagon, Chardon sat. He wore a green tunic and matching leggings, and the Lieutenant answered to him. Chardon's wiry face smiled. As the personal assistant to the Prime Magus, Chardon had been charged with tonight's raid. The Lieutenant handed him the latest transgression of Prince Kalero Tremayne. He printed a pamphlet entitled: *The Equality and Liberation of the Dim.*

"Keep several samples of these for evidence and whatever else you find. There's enough in the wagon."

"And the rest sir," the Lieutenant asked.

"Burn it alongside the Printers' Guild manager. Treason is treason after all."

The Council of Nobles passed a law recently that no material could challenge the teachings of the Wizardrium. Chardon closed his eyes. They had finally found the place where Prince Kalero had his works printed, and with this latest offense, they would issue an arrest warrant for the prince.

In the past, Prince Kalero had been caught handing out pamphlets about his metaphysical insights into the workings of the Source, which contradicted the Academy of Magery and the sanctioned teachings promulgated by the Wizardrium. The Academy and Wizardrium taught differently about the origins of magick and natural law than Kalero. For them, the discovery of the Enlightened Will and how the Will fueled various aspects and properties of matter were different because they denied the Will required the Source. They also believed that the Mages manipulated nature to whatever end they desire up to and including the Will of the King, even if this meant disturbing the

5

balance and gift of creation itself. For them, nature was not creation; it had no Source. Instead, nature served them as they perceived it to be. Kalero had openly published several works these past two years, hastily readying them for the printing press before his elders could withhold them.

Professionally, he had paid the price. He had been a professor, accomplished in other areas of magickal research. He had penned several articles on how to enchant various metals, heal tissue with the addition of herbal properties all the while attacking Alluria's fixation on manufactured pharmacological remedies, which only sold "cures" for profit. He was censured by some academic societies in other Kingdoms, and the Wizardrium had urged him to recant his first book, calling it a "dangerous speculation" and "a work steeped in lies." The Academy of Magery demoted him to tutor. His colleagues would nod, every once in a while, in his direction, but clearly, he was playing with academic fire. His ideas had caught on in the more interesting salons and cafes around Alluria. These salons and cafes were filled with artists, poets, and the leisurely class of Dimmers born to privilege in the noble wizard Houses of Alluria but without the power. For these people, the idea that someone occupied lesser status because they were Dim seemed ridiculous. Being dim meant having no access to the power of the arts of Magick. The artists, however, protested on the grounds of social injustice, and their work had come under recent scrutiny of the Wizardrium.

First, Kalero published a *Treatise on the Interplay of Balance and Will: A Theistic Companion to Magickal Metaphysics*. In that treatise, Kalero explained the Source's nature derived from balance. In his next book, *Confessions of a Theistic Wizard*, Kalero criticized the manners in which magick was employed tyrannically in his own brother's Kingdom. In the magical world he had authored and defied the will of the Wizardrium, the ruling bodies of wizards, along with the Alluria's Ministry of Information, and of course, his very own brother.

Several Wizardslayers in their obsidian-like Hecatium armor and inlaid copper-like runes stood outside. They had piled most of Prince Kalero's manuscripts, and the guild manager pleaded for his life. A Wizardslayer bashed him in the face with his gauntlet. The man fell silent and compliant as they fixed him to a makeshift log surrounded by Kalero's manuscripts and chopped up chairs and tables from inside the guild hall. The Wizardslayers lit the fire; three torches tossed into the pile of lies. Chardon smiled again and laughed as the print manager awoke to the flames at his feet. Chardon delighted in the agony before him. His master would be pleased.

Chapter 1

Dorn went out into the market. Allurian troops hammered a new ordinance about the new loyalty and sedition act. Next to those notices, Prince Kalero's face looked back in print. Scrawled atop the poster: Wanted. Dorn swallowed hard. Not to rouse any more suspicion, Dorn secured eggs, bread, and cheese from the local market and returned home the long way.

He went by the Printers' Guild Hall. Gerrin, the Printers' Guild Hall Manager's corpse dangled on a makeshift post locked by a chain. At the top of the post, a painted sign in blood read: Liar. Around the base, Dorn found burnt pages. There was enough to make out that these words were Prince Kalero's making.

Dorn did not sprint. Every urge in his body commanded him otherwise, but discipline and intelligence prevailed.

When he arrived back, he entered his house quickly. Isadora, his wife, approached him. "Best not to take long with such a simple thing as going to the market, hun. He's a prince at my

9

table." She mistook his nervousness for awkwardness as she grabbed the bag of food from him. Kalero sat joking with Naxon and Geru, their two sons. Kal felt at ease at Dorn's house. The home felt more like what a family should be, and he admired the awkward closeness in the brothers. The daughter Rigela sat across the way reading a history of Allurian architecture. Her flaxen hair lit amber by the morning sun.

"We need to talk," Dorn said almost commandingly and out of revered respect he held for his prince. The alarm in his voice startled Kal.

"What happened?" Kal asked. Isadora looked inquisitive.

"Take my memories. Now!"

Stretching out his two arms, Kal took Dorn's head in tenderness and friendship. Kal spoke words under his breath, his speech spidery making sounds that nobody in the room understood. Dorn offered no mental resistance. The spell was instant, and both Kal and Dorn fell into a shared consciousness like a friend dragging you into frigid lake. Images and thoughts coalesced merging into one awareness. In his mind, Kal walked with him inside the memories of the last hour. He saw the wanted poster, but more importantly, he saw the burnt pages at the feet of Gerrin's corpse. The sudden flash of concern for family, the guilt of serving his prince, and the dreams of a better tomorrow for all Vendans fading just like the sudden end to the spell. It ended there. The silence lingered between them, and ended with Kal putting scrolls and journals into his satchel with haste.

"What? What is it?" Isadora asked, her hands folded akimbo.

"Gerrin is dead. They burnt him in a pile of my writings, and now there's a warrant out for my arrest."

Kal continued to pack away his things. He had known Gerrin for the past four years.

Isadora pulled Dorn aside two rooms over. "He cannot stay here...Never again. They'll track him here. I just know it." She still held the ladle, which she used to emphasize her point.

"I know," Dorn said. He bit his lip. "At the same time, I can't just abandon my prince."

"The prince's life ended the moment the Council and Wizardrium deemed it as such."

"We're trying to make the world better," Dorn said.

"Dreams have a way of blinding dreamers. You have to get him out of here. By the blade, if you don't, I'll do it myself."

Dorn raised both hands. "I'll do it." He left Isadora in the room, and met Kal in the other room. "Sire, if…"

"I know dear friend," Kal rose from the chair. Rigela peered over her book watching the scene unfold not too sure about what exactly was happening, but she knew enough that Allurian architecture could wait. "I must leave tonight."

"Do you know where you will go my prince?"

Breathing in through his nose heavily, Kal shook his head negatively. "I have no idea where I am going." Flicking his wrist, both satchel and oakenwood staff floated to him. Naxon and Geru lighted up at the motion of objects floating through the air. "All that I do know is that to leave Venda would cause my critics to vilify me even more. If I face them, then I have a chance to finally be heard at the highest levels."

"Don't be naïve Kal. Whatever you do, make sure it's the right call. Many are not as enlightened as you regarding the Dim."

"I promise. I'll make this right."

Dorn's wide shoulders and copper-skin arms flexed as both hands embraced the smaller mage's biceps. "I know you will."

Flight of the Ravenhawk

Smiling, Kal eyed him with the longing wish that Dorn was his brother. Unfastening his cloak on a hook by the door, Prince Kalero pushed down on the thickly hinged door. Street lamp orbs emanated and poured into the lowly-lit den, and Kalero walked into the dark of night. As he left, Isadora bit her nails nervously, and Dorn slunk back into the chair. They did not speak the rest of the night.

Two hours later, Prince Kalero Tremayne entered the Wizardrium and asked to see his brother. The Wizardslayers took him into custody, and placed him under house arrest in the palatial wing. A day later, several wizards placed a force field of blue energy on that wing. Two days later, a tribunal summoned Prince Kalero.

****

The ticking clock clicked and chimed. Kalero Tremayne, a young man of thirty years and copper-skin sat in the comfy armchair. His satchel draped at his side, and his oakenwood staff hovered as his other hand swooshed it about in sync with his gesturing. Behind the desk, the young female swallowed at the display of gestural power, a fate and ability rarely seen in someone as young as Kalero. Unlike his colleagues, with whom power could only be casted by invocation of the High Art's true speech, the very language of what Kalero called "creation," Kalero could embody his will into movement. He could infuse the power of his will with the very magick he called the Will of the Source throughout the movements of his body. For him, the Source was the one true emanation of power in this universe, and he dared to call it the Light of God in his scholarship and teaching at the Academy of Magery. Beyond gestural wizards, the highest wizards casted from pure thought where no speech or gesture were needed to invoke the power wizards possessed.

Today, he had come willingly, hoping to shock his older brother out of apathy and the lust for power that consumed his soul. For his brother only two years older, unlike himself, had studied the High Arts of Magick all his life to achieve his talents, and while still young, Kalero could almost best him. Unlike Kalero, the King had simply done what he wished with his talent, as every wizard did. And this is what Kalero's latest pamphlet took issue with: Wizards using their power indiscriminately regardless of its effect on the balance of all things, and he also called attention to the systematic discrimination of the Dim. Wizards referred to those without magick as Dimmers or being dim, but are not like those beings of the Underdark that serve the will of higher darker forces. Unlike Kalero, King Darnashi had never answered to anybody, and now with their Father dead, the Allurian Kingdom knew great prosperity, but only at the expense of the Dim, the imbalance to nature due to Alluria's wizards, and the continual mistreatment entailed by such indiscriminate power—at the very least this was what the thesis of *Exploitation of the Dim and Other Effects of Rampant Power* contested.

Kalero had been a thorn in the side of the Academy for the past five years. No longer content with his station to merely observe as a learned man often does in the ivory tower, he went about trying to change the world through the pen. He started to write political pamphlets. With that, he could affect change, and hopefully make others see his point. He could use rational argument, the pen, and his mind to change the world for the better. That's why he never resisted and came straight here. He did not expect the Ministry of Information or the Prime Magus of the Wizardrium to call for a formal tribunal. Dean Smythe, though, had been a friend of his father, and so he rested his hope on that friendship. *Today could be different; today, I'll make them see how wrong they are*. His thoughts were hopeful. It had to work. His brother had to see it, and he'd get his big brother back, his *Nash*. King Darnashi would fall away, and he'd get his brother back.

While other rival kingdoms trade, and vie for power through trade, the Allurians had instituted magick for their benefit five centuries ago. The call for all nobles to be magick-users led to the inbreeding of wizard families to consolidate their power. Since that time, the pool did not thin, but diversified. Where inbreeding results in poor genes, the Allurians married anyone of magickal ability regardless of race. Those convinced of acquiring more magickal power did not care about the pretensions of the outside world. Now other magickally ensouled wills marry other magickally ensouled wills, and political allegiances within the Allurian Kingdom are not based on wealth of powerful noble houses as one might do by marrying off one's daughter. In Alluria, primogeniture was antiquated. Both women and men possessed assets and magickal power, but most importantly magickal power. The Allurians found that wealth is a byproduct of mastering the High Arts of Magick, and this mastery ensures the survival of one's house. As such, if one is noble, but not inclined to the wizardry arts, one might as well be an outcast, or be sent into some trade or service to the family by studying law or being appointed to some office in the Kingdom that can help with the more mundane affairs of revenue and influence. Kal's writings about the Allurian Kingdom was to pull its justification and hierarchy right out from under its feet.

A bell sounded above the young secretary's head, and she nodded. "They're ready for you." She swallowed hard.

Kalero sighed heavily. He summoned the courage of his heart to speak his mind, and to walk in with what little dignity he had preserved. He turned his staff sideways, and placed his satchel to hang from the minor enchantment as it floated behind him. As he walked past the secretary, she looked up at him "Best of luck sire. You were always my favorite, between you and your brother, I mean."

Returning her gaze, he smiled. "With the compassionate heart, comes the grace of the Source. It means a lot to me." Her hand brushed down his arm unconsciously like an estranged lover understanding that she would never see Kal again. Did she know something that he did not? He turned his head, puzzled.

Folding his hands behind his back, he waved the staff to follow him. Tick, tock, the clock chimed. Kalero looked into a mirror outside the Tribunal doors and ensured his black leather vest shined, and his shorter black hair was pulled neatly to the side from his more traditional part. He composed himself ensuring the sincerity of convictions, and stepped forward exhaling his last breath. Under their own power, the doors parted. While this was not the ideal place, he dreamt of the day he could share his ideas in a forum. He just didn't expect his ideas to land him into so much trouble, so quickly.

Dean Smythe sat off to the side raised on a mahogany platform that bore the legal seal of the Academy of Magery. Before him, Minister Gallafray scoffed at his physical presence, his knobby nose sucking all life and joy out of the room. To his left, the Prime Magus stood, a powerful man with lanky arms, white alabaster skin, and skull-sunken eyes like death itself. To his right and left, Wizardslayers grasped their enchanted polearms, and every once in a while, those polearms might sizzle with a blue arc of magical lightning. They wore the copper iron alloy of Hecatium, which could cancel and deflect magick. They readied their weapons at the young man. Kalero looked puzzled. Why the weapons? He first looked at Dean Smythe, who did nothing and said nothing. His eyes were empty like clear glass. Humiliation drained away any sincerity, and hope gave way to an uneasy panic.

"Mage Tremayne, second-born to your father King Hiraeus Tremayne of Alluria," said Minister Gallafray. "You've been brought before this tribunal to answer for crimes of denouncing the throne, a treasonous offense in itself were it not for your brother, the King. You also stand before the Wizardrium for separate crimes."

The Prime Magus cocked an eyebrow of uneasiness. "Mage Tremayne, you stand accused of spreading falsehood and misinformation against the very institution you represent as professor. Moreover, your seditious material also attacks the very pillars of wizardry in our society that preserves our way of life in the Kingdom, and the very crown of your family's legacy."

"Is that really what I have done? Prime Magus, Sir. Certainly, even if you do not regard the metaphysical origin of magick as I do, even if you see wizardry as a product of human will and nothing higher, certainly you must see that the way we work our craft has cosmic implications for non-humans, the environment, and spreads imbalance and injustice in the way we treat the Dim. Please. Don't do this. I only speak the truth in my own writings. If I could just…"

The doors burst open from behind him. "Enough!" a voice came from behind him. Kalero closed his eyes.

"I've heard it all before. I'd never expect that you'd betray the Kingdom with that last work of yours. Agents of the Wizardrium have already confiscated your book in several underground catacombs in the Neighborhood of Damask."

"The Lightdweller Temple. Please. Brother. Please tell me you did nothing to the worshippers," Kal said, exasperated.

Darnashi approached him, hands held behind his back. Darnashi's eyes widened in rage as he returned Kalero's gaze. "I did," Darnashi smiled, his lips parting his face in a wicked smile.

Kalero's breath became frantic and shortened pants of nervousness filled the room. Kalero fell over. His stomach churned like cement. All of those people, all the children, they had built a temple in the catacombs out of fear of persecution. Kalero told them he'd plead their case with the King—that is, when the time was right. He told them to stay in Venda and that eventually, they would be welcome. The Lightdweller Temple had circulated Kalero's books, and while Kalero had never come out and endorsed the Lightdweller religion, many knew of his sympathies, mostly due to his mother's own allegiance to the Lightdweller faith being tolerated in the royal family. King Hiraeus had declared that no harm come to the Lightdweller Church. Now, however, Darnashi had secured power and allegiances with the very powers Kalero thought himself safe from. Neither father nor mother were alive to constrain Darnashi's will; it had become tainted and vile. At this very moment, Kalero saw his naïve ignorance vanish revealing his brother's evil nature.

Everyone knew that the Academy was a bit freer than other sectors to write, share, and criticize the powers that be and his works were, as he saw them, academic treatises to be read by anyone with an active mind. Kalero felt that no work should go unread, even those he disagreed with personally. He still read them. Now, his ideas had gotten friends killed, the very friends that had helped him produce several hundred copies of his works. Kalero thought magick calls for wizards to only serve the Source, but never seek to alter the balance of creation. This proposition fits well into Lightdweller theology. Second, applying this principle to the Wizardrium would open magick up to people by serving them rather than reinforcing the privilege afforded to a few mages who hold onto power.

Third, the rampant abuse of magick is fairly evident in the city and natural world in which Allurians live.

"Your writings pose a threat to our family, our society, and the very establishment of wizardry itself. There's one way out. Otherwise, I'll sign the order to kill you myself."

"I'd listen to him if I were you, son," Dean Smythe suggested. "I'd hate for anything to happen to you." He put his face down immediately in shame. The word "son" burnt sharply in Kalero's mind. They had known each other all their lives.

"And what are the details of this way out?" Kalero spoke through his teeth, anger clenching his jaw.

The Prime Magus looked to the Minister who gestured for him to speak. "You will renounce your ideas publically in a letter, and before the entire Wizard Convocation swear fealty to your brother and the Wizardrium." He paused to pick his words carefully. "The Kingdom of Alluria cannot afford a split between the Wizardrium and the royal family."

Kalero scoffed, the bitterness of the gesture fairly evident. "The world is not fixed in terms of the values we can choose. We are free to create a better world, a world that does not exploit magick, but seeks to balance our relation to all beings."

"Platitudes of youth, even the young of thirty. I'd think twice before any more outbursts or attitudes. If you were anybody but the King's brother, you'd be facing the Wizardslayer's Axe!" Minister Gallafray said.

The tears of regret and loss overcame his rage for but an instant. Flickering flames danced on the walls, their unpredictable shapes looking freer than the trappings and biases of Kal's world crashing down upon him and his heart. The Damask neighborhood temple had been where Kal had met his friend Dorn, the man that ran the printing press, his family, and adopted daughter, Rigela.

"Brother, brother. Don't cry for them. They weren't wizards. They were Dim. Plain, clean, and simple Dims that worship the idea of magick all wrapped up in a myth."

In softened speech that revealed the twinges of loss and fury in the back of his throat, Kalero spoke. "Don't call it myth."

Darnashi had had enough. "Renounce your writings and this stupid faith of yours."

Forgetting Darnashi to be King, Kalero spoke looking straight at his brother, "Never."

His brother, also, forgot he was king, and ran his fist straight into Kal's flushed red face.

"Is that your final answer?"

Staggering back, Kal returned the gaze of an equal. "Yes."

"You realize what you're making me do."

"It's your decision not to listen to our mother, to see the throne before family. To defy father's wish that Lightdwellers like any religion be welcome in the Allurian Empire. That's your call. Not mine."

"They're dead Kal. I too made a promise to mother. I promised mother to keep you safe. You'd rather fall on the sword of your own beliefs and ideals than the family you should be helping!" Darnashi grabbed him by the collar.

"Helping? You're joking...Seriously, what happened to you Nash? Where'd my big brother go? What greed and power lurks in your heart that you throw away the sacred gift of creation itself? Why would you dishonor mother and father this way? Killing an entire community...women and children. Wizardry's a gift, a gift to serve others. You should've let them be. You should've kept them alive. They never *did* anything to us."

Flight of the Ravenhawk

Darnashi punched him in the face again, sending Kal onto his knees. Blood came from Kal's lip. He knelt over. The Minister shrugged to the Prime Magus, and the Prime Magus eyed both of them critically. Technically, they could do nothing. The King had taken on this matter for himself rather than hide behind the option they'd given him. "You're no brother of mine, not to me. Kill him." *Kill him?* The words rang hollow in the air. Kalero couldn't believe them, and he stared dumbfounded at his brother's words.

The Prime Magus smiled at the outcome. I couldn't have planned it better. The troublesome rat will end his own fate.

"What? Nash?" Kal protested.

"Make him suffer…a lot!" King Darnashi motioned to the two guards.

In one breath, be calm as water. In his mind, the magick buzzed. His finger rotated ever so slightly beyond notice catching the tiny threads of magick he prepared prior to the meeting. *Never let a wizard* as the old Allurian saying went. In mind and hand, Kal held a magick that tasted like salt water on his tongue, but held the power of a tidal wave. Kal punched the ground, and the floor swelled with magick. Both staff and Kal fell through a whirlpool of water to the level below leaving his accusers above the castle granite floor. His tears became the gateway. He entered what looked to be open offices of the Wizardrium. On the far wall, a large window faced the city.

As water splashed around him, a desk broke his fall and the ceiling returned to stone. An elderly lady pushed her spectacles up. She eyed him in surprise as water covered her hair and papers on the desk. "Oh dear," she said looking at the fallen prince rising from her desk.

"Excuse me," he politely said. The woman could only nod back. She knew the prince, and apparently, the whole room knew him.

"Everybody, stand back." The entire room did as they were told.

He pointed one arm to the left, and his staff to the other as he parted the desks before a strip of windows. A wall of force shot out and the glass shattered. In his hands, the magick felt raw, untamed, and wilder than ever before. It leapt out of him, flashing with his anger that fueled it. He sprinted out to the ledge, and jumped out. In a flash, his brother materialized from above. However, he was too late. Kal was already on the horizon fleeing. There was no warning that Kal could work a spell without speaking. This ability was something Kal never really spoke about aloud to others, yet even the Dim office workers knew what they saw that day. For the whole meeting, he'd been preparing this spell and the next. He didn't really think now. His heart felt the weight of betrayal. His brother was truly lost.

In his mind, Kal spoke a spell of changing. He infused his name with the ravenhawk. The power came only from him, a draining affair. The power came through him like the torrent of water magick before except in this changing, he brought sadness and urgency into the working. His emotions fusing the magick, holding it there as his mental mind chanted words of changing and making, and he altered himself, burying the true name of ravenhawk into his very soul and being. He drew in his entire form, incorporating them into the changing as well.

As he fell through the air, his staff floated behind him, his leather satchel secured on it. In the air and in the fall, the staff had attached itself to his back forming black-feathered wings. Kal brought into his shapeshift form his belongings. Transformed into a ravenhawk, Kal sped away into the condemnation of daylight, his flight enhanced by the speed of enchanted winds and an undying rage in his heart.

From the window, Darnashi looked out to the black speck in the azure sky. The Prime Magus approached him from behind, "Orders?"

"Declare my brother a traitor. Send out your agents and best slayers. Kill him on sight if I should fail this day." The Prime Magus nodded and said nothing to King Darnashi.

Raising his arms, Darnashi activated the magick of his obsidian-like armor. The magick in the armor tasted like ash from a volcano. In Darnashi's head, a trapped and dying dragon soul cried out silent muffles in every working of the enchanted armor. Darnashi's armor morphed into spikes and scales. Arms changed into leathery wings. Boiling his insides, Darnashi could feel the blood of dragon's course through his veins, burning like cinders landing on skin. Everywhere his muscles stretched, bones breaking and re-knitting underneath undulating skin. Kal looked back, his acute ravenhawk eyesight saw Darnashi's form morphing in air behind him. Hovering in midair, Darnashi had become an armored black-like obsidian dragon, birthed from rage and imbuing his armor with the actual lifeforce of a dragon long slain for the purpose of power. Sacrificial magick was unholy, and a sad realization dawned on Kal. His brother was gone.

Flight of the Ravenhawk

Had he been so blind to his brother learning how to imbue and sacrifice the life essence of a dragon in his armor? Had Kal been so engrossed in his studies he failed to see his brother's heart and rise to power? Or had he always been dark? Had he really gone to such necromantic depths of the Underdark itself? Where had he secured a dragon to sacrifice it and imbue into the armor he wore?

Carried by invoked magickal winds, ravenhawk-Kal felt the bespelled winds hurl him farther than ravenhawk wings could, yet the massive enchanted wings of the dragon form would soon overtake him, especially in open sky. If Kal let fear in, it would hinder the focus on the spell. Shapeshifting was a funny art. If the shapeshifter anthropomorphized his own self while in a shapeshifted form for too long, the mage runs the risk of losing that form. A bird who feared and felt too long would become man, falling to his death. Unlike a bird, the dragon was a sentient creature. Darnashi could think and react as himself with absolute freedom because dragons were sentient in that form already. Kal let the bird take over even more. Trusting in the Source for his power, the bird had one thing that Darnashi the man-dragon did not. Instinct.

J. Edward Hackett

Kal touched on his instinct, the part that meditated consciously to become unconscious. There, in that space of spiritual practice, he found the no-mindedness to let the ravenhawk take over. He counted the wing beats, the primal instinct of fear, and tried to find the balance. The ravenhawk flew back into the structures of the city. *Hide. Don't flee.* Darnashi fell behind him as Kal banked sharply upward. The dragon could not bank up in such short spurts, and fell slightly, increasing the distance between ravenhawk and dragon. The dragon hit the roof broad on the left shoulder sending rocks and debris on the people below. Yet, it wasn't enough. The impact only enraged the beast. The hawk swooped circular around a castellated tower of the city guard keeping low to street level, and Darnashi was forced to pull up again, enraged. The dragon could not fit in the city. Giving Kal time he was losing his focus. Again, he was thinking too tactically. Trying to find the oneness of that form before, he breathed again. Restoring his form Kal flew into the water canal while Darnashi's huge form loomed above watching his prey from a distance. The dragon hurled a stream of lightning. Intense heat sparked behind the ravenhawk searing water, steam, and stone.

Flight of the Ravenhawk

Fear overcame Kal, and in one instant when the canopy of the marketplace covered the ravenhawk's flight before the Eastern Gate Market, Kal became man once more. The big iron doors bearing the crest of dragon and ravenhawk loomed behind them, openly divided on each side, poetically expressing the conflict coming to fruition as terrified citizens watched in horror. Prince Kalero was now in human form, running underneath the canopy of market tents pushing people out of his way waving staff in hand. Behind him, King Darnashi's voice boomed thunderous as he stomped on the populace urgently trying to find Kal. Snickering, the dragon realized the plan. He swooshed his huge wings and hovered before the Eastern Gate. He breathed lightning melting their hinges as Kal came out of the gap between the tent line as the doors collapsed.

"Coward," the dragon-Darnashi hissed.

"Murderer," somehow Kal had the strength of will to point and stare at the creature. "These are your true colors. Aren't they brother?" Several of the Allurians looked on in horror and fascination. The dragon form engenders a primal fear in all lesser beings who are sentient. Such primal fear can lure you or frighten you to flee. Animals know better than to tangle with a dragon. Wizards, though, they never learn.

"Indeed. It has come to this, Kal. I promise to make it quick," the dragon roared.

Kal centered himself. He'd never been in battle before. Though most wizards are taught to keep composure in the heat of the moment, most of the Allurian mages led privileged lives where conflict never found them. They were more scholar-politicians and wizard-entrepreneurs who fused magick with their clockwork machinations. *Can't fly, can't fight.*

A devilish grin of malignant mockery parted Darnashi's face. "It's good to be King."

"Good? What you? You've always been a joke." The people heard this. They heard Kal's defiance, and some of them could not help but gasp in shock. Darnashi said nothing. His face grimaced, dragon eyes piercing Kal's soul. Kal opened his magickal senses. A plan started to form. The timing had to be *perfect*.

Darnashi shot his lightning breath. Instinctively, Kal reached out for the solid metal door with a spell of force. Ripping it from its gigantic hinges, Kal levitated it between Darnashi and himself. It shielded him, but the protection couldn't last. Sparks erratically jumped from the door's center. Within twenty seconds, the metal melted off like dripping molten ice as Darnashi sprayed his lightning breath weapon with fury. Kal had to do something. Stepping to the side of the shield-door and with magickal force and prayer, his magick shot the door to one-side of the dragon's unfurled wing. Unpracticed in this form, Darnashi tried to get out of the way, but Darnashi still thought as a human. Like thickened blood, several gooey pieces of molten iron landed all over his torso, face, and the wing's membrane. Off balance and too late, Darnashi brought his claw to shield his face, and staggered back as lava-like steel covered segments of the reflective pools of polished dragon scales. The door did not have to land with force to crush his brother. Kal needed only to wound him.

Staggering, Darnashi ran forward knocking over several structures in the process— his dragon scaled flesh burning. Kal fled into the fortified doorway and tunnel. Darnashi hissed with fury and lunged his wounded body towards Kal. Then, Kal pulled the portcullis down as Darnashi's head and torso entered the tunneled Eastern Gate underneath. Metal spikes impaled Darnashi's shoulder, and Darnashi shifted back into human form. Severe burns covered his face, left arm, torso, and his left leg lay crushed by a segment of portcullis spike and a small pool of crimson started to encircle him. Had he not shapeshifted so fast, Darnashi would be dead. Their eyes met. Kal was filled with regret. Darnashi's eyes knew only hatred and pain, a wounded animal more so now than in dragon form, and infinitely more dangerous.

For a second longer than life itself, the brothers locked gazes. In the distance, the Wizardslayers were on his heels, and Kal knew he could not stay. While powerful, Kal could not defeat entire legions now screaming in unison, and having foregone a lifetime of politics for academics he had no allies to take back and restore the Allurian Empire. Above, a skyship loomed sending many armored Wizardslayers on floating vehicles to defend their King.

As soon as Darnashi blinked, Kal was back in the ravenhawk form. Fast, hard, and away, from the door emblazoned with the ravenhawk still stood, the dragon door rested underneath it shattered into pieces.

Chapter 2

The ravenhawk flew on spell winds for three weeks. Kal zigzagged this way and that, trying to confuse those that followed, if they did at all. Kal had spent much of his power flying, and without sufficient strength, he could become trapped in this form forever. The ravenhawk's eyes were more powerful and acute than human vision. Kal shed a tear for the brief seconds he flew over the Allurian Capital, Venda. He saw the neighborhood of Damask, the burnt bodies and mangled stones left in the wake of mage fire. He knew his brother had been lustful for power. He could not imagine that his brother would join up so easily with the Wizardrium, and even more to the point, he felt guilty, guilty about being so naïve. The ideas, the scholarship, these were meant to taper the Wizardrium, to call for its reform, empower the Dim against the Wizards that served nobody but themselves, and preserve the aims of peace. All his work, all his time, they were meant for something more than the end he was living out now. These thoughts came to him, overwhelming his attention to the spell. The ravenhawk flew into the canopy below searching for something to eat. Regret and guilt turned him back into a human, and Kal brought his form down into the tree line. He felt the lashes and cuts of branches as he fell, tumbling down into the ferns of the forest floor his human body exhausted. Everything went dark.

Caressing his face, the sun of new day's mist warmed him. He could feel a bruised rib cage and many cuts and bruises on his arms and legs. Slung across his chest, his satchel hung and nearby, he found his staff. He ached to walk. He would need to shapeshift again soon with the wizardslayers fast on his heels if they were coming. Had he flown North, South, East, or West? He could not tell. With the new day sun, he reached for its warmth and its sublime beauty. So much beauty in the world, so much beauty made intelligible by the Source since only in relation to the Source does any of it mean something. He had to stop being distracted by some inane philosophical wonder. It had blurred his vision of the very freedom he thought he had as second-born, and the price his ideas had cost him and others was staggering. Looking up in prayer, he could not tell where he was to go, nor what the Source had in store for him, if anything at all.

Flight of the Ravenhawk

Leaning on his staff, Kal hobbled about. He opened his mage eyes to the energies around him, and found life coalescing around a babbling brook. Here, Kal would stop. Stop and rest amidst the turmoil of the world. Arms ached. Cuts singed at the touch of a passing leaf. Stop and rest he thought to himself. In the forest, healing magick came easier. Saying words aloud that nobody should hear, Kal worked a spell on his body and let the slow acting healing spell work its way through his system. He whispered the quiet words of mending, took two handfuls of cold spring water, and fell asleep.

Hobbling, Kal leaned on his staff. His need called out to it, and the magick snapped out of him, nearly knocking himself over. As he caught it, he winced in pain. Cuts and bruises adorned his copper skin, and he wiped his unbathed matted hair from his face. He leaned on a tree, satchel still slung across his chest, staff in hand. He held fast to his mother's pendant, still there and reassuring. With the sun overhead, he walked aimlessly, footfalls heavy as his burdened heart. In the forest, he was alone much like in his beloved city. He walked alone; his brother consumed. Kal shed tears as he walked. By sunfall, he saw an abandoned cabin. The pain in his legs was unbearable and aching, but the pain was deeper, disappointing, and for the first time, Kal had nobody.

"Hello," he managed to scream, his voice barely able to escape the newly formed human throat while his mind still very much caught in the dissipating magick of his ravenhawk form. Nobody. He could not manage more than that, and even then, his words came out cawing like a raven. Nobody returned his words, nobody to hear the screams of his anguished heart and the day his family and city died to him. Cast aside and unwanted, the abandoned cabin looked as if built by human hands, yet morphed out of the ground by elven ecomancers, a fusion of human pragmatism and elven tradition.

Kal hopped up the stairs, leaning on his staff. "Hello" he managed again. The forest answered in silence and bird calls. The door was unlocked. All windows inside were sealed, curtains drawn, and linens covered furniture. The hearth cold with abandoned wood. A bedroom was recessed in another room, but stooped down into another level as if swallowed by earth and wood; it looked used. Whoever lived here would be back. Kal came outside, deciding not to upset a potential host, and found the wooden porch as good enough as any place to fall. Partially covered by the elements, Kal slept. Strength, magick, and vitality returned slowly.

The velvet curtain of night came suddenly; it brought a stark coldness. Instinctively, Kal wrapped himself in his shirt. In his delirium, he saw a feminine figure. She was hidden in dark greens, a cloak concealing gentle cheeks. She breathed the smell of honey and vinegar, her words elven, soft, and fluid. "Sleep," she spoke, and a waterfall of magick and fireflies came out of her. He felt his copper skin burn and then soothe like the gentle first gust of a door opened onto winter. In fact, he felt his body awash in snow and warmth. Shivering gave way to warmth, and then the dreaming. His brother pursued him, and he ran for a night unsure of himself. In the back of his mind, however, he knew the smell of honey and vinegar lingered somewhere.

In the morning, Kal awoke. His reserve of magick pressed on his head like the assurance of a sheathed sword. Kal knuckled his eyes, and rose on a couch. The hearth burnt, and the smell of fresh stew rose from a tiny pot, just enough for one person. Someone had taken him inside, he realized. His staff leaned against the wall, satchel hung on hook next to it, and his shirt, leggings, and vest were neatly washed and folded on the end table before him. In a small bowl, a soothing salve had been applied to bruises and cuts all over his body. Too modest, Kal jerked the blanket up to see that he lie naked and sighed heavy with embarrassment. He reapplied what remained of the salve and felt the coolness in his skin, and the aching of his legs soon left.

"Hello," he called out. "Is there anyone here?" He dressed and went to the porch. "Hello," he called gently in every direction and up. In new day's light, he felt rejuvenated, and the forest returned gentle breezes of warmth and bird song like before. The stew bubbled over, now. Whoever his host, they left the stew and portion for himself only. In the kitchen, a note read: *Eat*. Again, he looked around. A loaf of bread sat cooling with a towel draped over it. The bread and stew went down swiftly—the type of meal that stuck to his ribs giving comfort and strength. He drank the remaining broth, and washed it down with a tea kettle that also hung over the fire.

He warmed his hands by the fire and felt the wash of heat overtake him. An idea occurred to him. His hands caught that warmth and the hospitality of his absent host. He held that feeling in his hand, and began to summon the true name of fire and time. The magick came quickly, but more controlled. For some time, he knitted fire and time together in an intricate lacing, etching the magick into the very stone of hearth. The magick felt like ambers and a nice cedar burning and for a long comforting time, Kal held it in his hands before letting it go. Once he did, the etched runes appeared in stone, chiseled out in the very working, and the magick tasted like the memory of the stew and tea. Moving his arms about, Kal washed the whole cabin aglow in his magick, the cedar smell now on the tongue as he spoke more words.

Finding the ink quil and pen on a nearby counter, he wrote back to his mysterious host:

Dear Host,

Your hospitality has known the company of a wizard. I do not know how long I lie in your home, but rest assured, I give back what I can. The hearth is now enchanted. The fire will always appear when needed and as needed without need of timber. I have warded the entire cabin to never catch fire. You will always be as warm and safe as you treated me.

Thank you.

He did not sign his name.

In the trees above, the Elven Druid, Sylvara looked down, pushing back the silvery mane of hair for which she was no doubt named.

Her hair fell straight and shimmered like a waterfall of moonlight. Her purple eyes saw that Kal was different than all others. For one thing, he was calm, almost serene if it were not for the wincing pain. The human had fallen, embarrassingly mid-spell, yet she could sense the workings of magick in him without the faintest sign of spoken word or gesture. She saw him leave the cabin and walk into the forest. On silent heels, the trees lifted her, and she followed him from above.

In these forests, he would soon be discovered by the patrols. Holding his side and hopping, Kal trumped about like a buffoon, staff clanging on ancient unearthed roots, and he made no effort to conceal his location. Though healed and restored, he was not graceful. Unbeknowst to Kal, he landed in the Ancestral Wood, sacred home and land of the elves. While these woods were travelled, none entered without express permission into the Ancestral Wood. Unlike others, he bore no weapons in the elven wood save a small dagger at his belt, which he undoubtedly had no martial training in. He cut down no tree to make a fire that day. Lowering himself on a log, he sought herbs on a nearby rock, which she knew to be for anti-inflammatory purposes. Kal ate them raw, and drew out a small wooden bowl from his satchel. He drank the water, and after that, he pulled his medallion from his neck.

Sylvara's eyes caught it as she did when she undressed him back in the cabin. At first, it had shocked her. Then, her curiosity got the better of her. The medallion was silver set against a black stone on a simple leather thong. Silver lines came to the center of the carved precious stone. Sharp, bright, and thin lines of the star were interspersed between four shorter points in between. In the Elven tradition, this was the star of Galadrana, the womb of the Goddess Queen and creator of all life, even the lesser human races. If the human was anything, he might be a Lightdweller, a sect of humans that claimed, like the elves, that everything must be in balance. Instead of the Goddess Queen, the humans claimed it was from the Source, an abstraction of Galadrana. However, the last Lightdweller and mage she'd seen had come when she was just a child of 15. Aged in her mid 170s, that encounter had been over a century and a half ago before the human kingdoms hunted down and distorted Lightdweller teaching. Could this human be the genuine thing? Even the medallion would cause the approaching patrol to pause. She motioned for them to keep their distance. As the Elven

King's daughter, she had privilege to command them even if she lived apart from Zalanthas in her own forest dwelling.

****

Out of nowhere, four elven archers were upon him while he sat against a large spruce tree fallen from storm winds. They bore the leather armor of Zalanthas, and immediately Kal knew where he had landed. *The ancestral wood, sacred home of the forest elves of Zalanthas.* Keeping his hands on his chest, he opened his eyes.

"I did not know where I fell. I mean no offense."

Saying nothing, the patrol never flinched and Kal wondered if they understood Basic. They waited for Princess Sylvara. She emerged in deadly silence. Leaning on a hefty ancient oak, she bit into an apple, her form unreadable save for the elven green cloak draped over her. "A little lost, human."

"If you only knew the half of it. You can come down, elf." Kal said gesturing to the patrol. "Clearly, I am outnumbered." He closed his eyes and put his head back against the tree. The four elven archers looked at her and communicated in gesture their readiness. She waved them off signaling her intent not to harm. Lowering their bows, they still kept an arrow notched.

It had been some time since she used the human speech known as basic. "How do you know it's safe to close your eyes?"

"Because, if you wanted me dead, you'd have killed me by now." Opening his eyes, he looked up from the ground and finished his water. "Besides, I think one of you was my benevolent host."

Sylvara cocked her head smiling. "Yes, yes I was."

"Where are my manners?" He could feel the bruises and pain waning, but he needed more rest. He hobbled up, and used the tree to brace himself as he rose. For now, he empowered what strength he might need by drawing on his own internal energy.

"Probably left with your dignity back there in that tumble you took, dear sir."

"You saw that, huh." Kal's smile stretched with embarrassment. "Not my most graceful moment."

Kal smiled at her wit. He hadn't chuckled or felt the tinge of warmth from someone else in a while. When he had composed himself, he bowed perfectly, his posture consistent with Elven decorum. "Greetings of the Goddess Queen's scepter. I am Kalero Tremayne."

"Your Elvish; it's perfect," she said mesmerized by his almost flawless and formal Elven not commonly known by any human, even traders.

"It is proper upon receipt of the scepter's touch from the Goddess Queen that another return the greeting with due haste." Kal returned with equal wit.

"Yes, yes. Of course." She regained her eloquent elven composure. He knew their ways too. "I am Sylvara daughter of Vanaxx Quintoriel." She bowed with due respect, and the archers saw the greeting.

"I take it I flew South then to Zalanthas and the claimed territory of the Elven Wood, held and ruled over by King Quintoriel."

"You did. I would think we've already covered this. By the large great bows all around you," Sylvara mocked.

"And I am trespassing on elven soil?"

"You are."

"And you are also his daughter?"

"I am," she smiled.

"And I trespassed in your cabin?"

"You did."

"Then you should know, as I explained in the note, I am a wizard and that your hearth will never need timber for it ever again. I have enchanted it and lay wards around your home of protection that you would know the safety and warmth as you treated me," Kal said.

Kal changed the pitch of the accent of some words and changed his inflection of the nouns in his speech reflecting the fact that he was talking to someone highborn. "I put your kingdom in terrible danger. I wish safe passage through the Ancestral Wood, even escorted if you like, but I must make haste. Wizardslayers follow me." She cocked an eyebrow in amazement. He had mastered the protocols of highborn and lowborn elvish, too. She also noticed that he used the same protocols of speech in reference to himself. He must be highborn, too. Then, it hit her. Tremayne was the ruling family line of the Allurian Empire.

"Wait… Wizardslayers?"

"They hunt me."

"And a Lightdweller?" she pointed to the pendant.

"Yes," Kal said.

"Permission denied. We should seek the counsel of my father first."

Tensen spoke up from her retinue. "My Lord, do you think it wise to bring him into Zalanthas?"

"He does have a point. Danger follows me even now," Kal said. He clenched his teeth as he stood on his bruised leg and breathed shallow breaths as he held his side. The pain lessened though bothersome. The idea of seeing Zalanthas intrigued him, and the elves might not want him there in the first place.

Purple eyes glanced sideways into the forest. Sylvara rested her chin in her delicate hand, and paced back and forth. "Tensen's words are true." She walked some distance before turning around to pace back towards Kal, her eyes peering into the ferns at her feet. "Yet, you were also true. If the Goddess Queen ordained this meeting, then there is no accident that Princess and Prince meet in the Ancestral Wood. My father would want to hear of this. Still, Tensen's mind is tactical, and I always heed his counsel." Softly, her eyes met his own. "Can you wear a glamour about your person?"

Saying nothing, Kal nodded.

"Make yourself into someone indistinct that could be part of my guards. When we come in, it will appear as if I go to my father's house…Yes, that would work best. From there, mage prince, we'll do as my father instructs."

"Sounds like a plan to me, and before it's too late, thank you." Kal raised his arms as if to embrace heaven and life itself. From without, he sensed the magick in the very essence of life, as if the Goddess Queen herself had blessed him. Like last night, the magick in this place tasted like bird song and eternal spring. Sparkles of floating dust and streams of canopy piercing sunlight threaded together in Kal's hand gesture. He caught light and spoke its true name, calling it to him, coaxing it like an amber into flame. Kal's words and gestures knitted the light itself to form an illusion. The words were warm on his tongue. The light took features from all the guards present into a unique visage and blended together in ribbons caught in Kal's hands. Appearing as one of her guards, he matched the most common fair blonde hair, and his skin no longer copper-hued became as silken white as the blonde hair of her retinue. His face became longer, narrower, and his features now were more subtle, less ugly by human standards. In his hand, the staff became a bow, and the dull green cloak and outfit appeared to have all the trimmings of sword, quiver and backpack.

Tensen gasped, "You could be brother to anyone of us."

"I live to serve only ma'lady," Kal spoke. His freehand made a fist, and he brought it to left shoulder.

"Then again, maybe not." Tensen laughed and took up point as they began to walk.

Some moments passed as Kal walked next to Sylvara. Confused, Kal returned his gaze to her. "What did I do wrong?" he asked.

"It's the other shoulder. Salute me always with the left fist just under the right shoulder," Sylvara said as her eyes smiled for her. "Try not to do anything in relation to me at all when we enter the city. Finally, they don't speak unless I speak to them. When they speak, it's expected that my guards are allowed to use informal speech with me and me alone."

"Except if I were Tensen?"

Her eyes narrowed. "That's different."

****

As they walked, ancient trees jutted up from the ground like castle spires. Golden rays of midday light cascaded through the trees warming them as they walked. Shaped by immortal elven patience, gem-colored flowers, emerald vibrant ferns, and majestic cedar trees lined the path into the city. The very Ancestral Wood smelt of enchantment and possessed an aura of tranquilty unlike anything Kal knew. As they approached the city, the boundaries between the enchanted glens and architecture took a long time to spot. Unlike human stone, the elves forged balance between what they needed without creating imbalance in the life around them. Natural organic patterns of ornate geometry served as filigree on gates of shaped wood, windows, and doors. Staircases around the ancient trees emerged out of the wood, morphed by powerful elemental magicks and elven craftmanship. The cornices of the halls and rooms linking these wooden designs were sketched in the relief of ancient histories, elven script, and reliefs of the elements. As they walked, every archer from the Ancestral Wood came in with Sylvara. A procession grew around her and in that spectacle nobody took notice of the fifth elven guard in her retinue. At this attention, Sylvara either didn't notice or care. She had not been back for some thirty years, a while even for the long-lived forest elf. Her return seemed to agitate the stoic presence of elves Kal had read about.

Several daughters of the noble Houses lined the streets. They openly gawked at Sylvara. Curling their arms around their children, several mothers pulled back their children from her brisk pace. Through it all, Sylvara trotted along with grace and determination one expected of House Quintoriel. Several of the lowborn elves stared at her; some made faces of disgust and disapproval. In these faces, Kal saw the same human contempt

Allurian mages held for the Dim. What had she done?

For an hour, they continued in silence marching through the forested avenues of Zalanthas before coming upon what Kal thought to be another residence of another highborn. The mansion was simple, yet elegant. A massive staircase parted the front entranceway from both sides. A massive stained-glass window loomed above cascading light in purples, greens, reds, blues, yellows, and orange. The symmetrical pattern of the light resembled the elven world tree, and the throned Goddess Queen holding her scepter in one hand and a book in the other. The archways looked like teardrops of dried and often stained wood. Glass panes were organic, never the same shape, not cut like the imperialist design of Allurian glass. Elven glassmakers, immortal in skill, carved and grinded the glass as if their art contained magick.

In an adjacent room, an old elf with seamless white hair flowed like waterfall to the floor. He sat atop a throne wearing a crown made of antlers and carved wood framed in simple gold etchings. An eye of suspicion came over him as he saw, for the first time in some thirty years, his daughter enter the throne room. Several of the royal guard fell in line behind her, including Kal.

Without speaking, the King dismissed them, and they seemed to follow his orders without question. Only one lingered.

"I motioned for you to leave," the King repeated. He found the glamour convincing.

Sylvara peered over at him, her eyes never leaving the very convincing illusion. "Forgive me." The sparkling dust shimmered about his person; the bow quickly returned into a staff of oakenwood. Kal's appearance was himself again—copper-hued skin and matted black hair tied in a slight ponytail. A long, weathered face wore fatigue like sword bore dents in the blade. "My name is Kalero Tremayne, Prince of Alluria."

In elvish custom, the traveler announced their intention. One is given a day to make this request. As it still was the first day, King Vanaxx had no choice but to hear what Kal had to announce to them.

"Speak," he ordered Kal.

"As I said, my name is Kalero Tremayne, second-born to King Hiraeus Tremayne of the Allurian Kingdom. I am a Lightdweller and wizard. I seek passage through Zalanthas, the Ancestral Wood, and adjacent claims to King Vanaxx Quintoriel. I need only modest provisions, but make no mistake. Some

53

haste is needed as I am pursued by the Crown for matters of treason. These are not affairs I would trouble you with, sire and they are problems that do not involve the elves. I came here by mistake, and I should leave as quickly as I made that mistake. The Wizardslayers are at my back, and I'd prefer not to bring them here. Your daughter thought it no accident we met, and so counseled that I come here to speak with you about these matters."

"I am King Vanaxx Quintoriel, Steward of the Wood. You confess to a crime to a nearby Lord? While there are no treaties, I'd expect Allurian nobles would make some claim that I am obliged to tell them of you and your whereabouts."

"At the request of your daughter, I wore a glamour about my person, concealing my identity as we entered. Nobody knows me here except for those present." Kal looked about the room.

Vanaxx chuckled. "My daughter is wise…sometimes."

Ignoring her faither's comment, Sylvara gazed at him starkly. The human was rather blunt. She suspected he had no tact and that deceit was not in his nature, which might make him a great wizard but a terrible prince. Still, she suspected that, like other humans, Kal might lead them astray. There was a saying in their world common to many tongues. *Never mince words with a wizard.* Just because he seemed not to lie directly doesn't mean that as a wizard Kal might omit some details. Wizards had barbed tongues. They concealed what they didn't think others should know.

"Why tell me any of this this?"

"He is mage and Lightdweller," Sylvara confessed. She pointed to the medallion, and silence fell over Vanaxx's stoic face. They had announced him as such, but he'd hardly given it a passing glance. At the sight of the medallion, he was stunned. The last time he saw that medallion the humans and elves lived in peace, and now they lived only in relative indifference after the border skirmishes.

"My eyes deceive me? Not too many of those around anymore."

"Yes, this one belonged to my mother," Kal said.

Vanaxx stroked his beard downward, and for an instant, his green silken robe caught the light with his motion. "Was your mother's name Enayra?"

"Yes," Kal said enthusiastically, thinking that there was some reason why he was led here.

"Your mother was friend to House Quintoriel. She helped as a healer when war between Alluria and the Knight Mages almost came to its full force. There were several skirmishes with equal losses on both sides, but no side fielded an army. Then Hiraeus saw her when visiting my Court under the banner of suggested peace. It was their union that halted the advance and progression of Alluria's claim to the resources in these woods. She taught you elven no doubt."

Kal nodded. "I'm a good study." Vanaxx smiled softly. His heart warmed at the knowledge that Enayra's son stood before him.

Vanaxx rose from his throne. Effortlessly, he walked, almost gliding. As he approached, Kal could see his fair skin, grainy as if made of wood, and reflective as if polished. His many years in the sun weathering his face to somewhere near the upper age of eighteen centuries or so.

"Walk with me." Vanaxx opened a door into his private study adjacent to the throne room "I know you are a good study. The Lightdwellers thrive outside of Venda, and while you may be aware of your infamy in the halls of Venda and the Academy of Magery…Do I have that correct? You were at the Academy?"

"Yes, I am a tutor there." He paused. "At least, I was. How did you know?"

"Several Lightdwellers brought your writings here," Vanaxx gestured with an open hand at several copies of Kal's books. They were strewn about a table in scholarly clutter on the study's desk. "I've ordered elven editions of these works as they moved me so. No human writing about balance and the Source has ever captured the very way magick was entrusted to us. Your insight into these matters is, shall I dare say, very elven!"

Kal smiled.

He was speechless. He never expected that his writings had made it very far out of the city. He felt rather obscure, lost in his studies, writing for audiences that neither cared nor liked what he wrote. During his life, he was only told that he must continue to write, possibly teach, but to stay alive, he must publish. At the Academy of Magery, his students were all power-hungry, thinking that magick would be a way to advance their station, Noble House, and a force worked against the Dim. For them, magick was a way to seek power rather than harmony. Kalero

J. Edward Hackett

Tremayne had stepped on toes, calling into question the very basis on which magick had been perceived in the very hall of power from which he had come. This was no small thing, though his mother would tell him only speak the truth and follow his heart, the heart entrusted to him by the Source. So he had written what he thought would be his magnum opus: *Treatise on the Interplay of Balance and Will: A Theistic Companion to Magickal Metaphysics*. It was bound in white-stained leather and azure blue with green and purple stones cast in the binding. Under it, Kal could only glimpse his more informal reflection, *Confessions of a Theistic Wizard*, his musings on the normative evaluations of the social, political, and ethical framework of the Allurian elite. It was bound in white with gold letters etched into a tanned leather frame.

"I was only publishing these writings through an underground Lightdweller temple in the neighborhood of Damask." His eyes lit up. "You had contact with them, or at least some people that knew them." Vanaxx's smile reassured him, following the mental thoughts out from premise to conclusion. There might be survivors! As the ravenhawk, he flew for weeks. In that form, three weeks passed, and the nervous

58

agitation in his eyes and on his lips spoke volumes to the elven lord. Vanaxx saw his train of thought, and nodded yes. Kal froze, the anticipation unnerving him and very visible.

"Several of the Damask survive in a human settlement in the woods of Zalanthas."

At that moment, Kal felt his hand close over the medallion. He whispered a prayer of thanks to the Source. He could feel the weight of purpose shining on him. He did not have to say anything. This place, this strange coincidence of mere escape, from being blown out of one place for another, Kal knew he had to be here. His vocation, his calling, his expulsion from the very institutions he wished to serve could offer him nothing, and his brother's love may have been never there at all. He'd been naïve to believe in his brother's potential to restrain his lust for power and that appeals to reason were even possible. And yet, there was also the hope. The hope of something more, something higher being moved in the spirit right between him, Vanaxx, Sylvara, and now news that some may have survived his brother's wrath. Kal did not ask, but expected that, like any King, Vanaxx had eyes and ears inside Venda, the capital. He would not press the issue.

"Tell me, if you can. There was a family. Dorn…"

Sylvara placed a hand on his shoulder with care and tenderness. "Dorn and his eldest, Rigela survive. They passed through the Lightdweller railroad in the ancestral wood a short time ago." As if he were human, Vanaxx half-smiled. Half a family—that's what Kal's ideas had cost: Half a family. At that, Kal could not help it anymore. He had stored up the rage, the disappointment, and the tragedy of escape for him and those who were massacred. The massacre of the Lightdwellers at Damask had been very personal.

In ravenhawk form, he swallowed that responsibility hard. The Tribunal and his brother surprised him that day. Never having time to process that loss, Kal remembered Isadora's worrisome face, her eyes concerned about the safety of her children. In his mind, he just recalled their names: Isadora, Naxon, and Geru. He knew them, and kept them close to his heart. He ate their soup; sung around the fire as the children danced to Dorn's proficient playing of the reed flute. Without thought, Dorn risked his life and operated the press. For days and nights, he printed Kal's writings. How many times had Isadora warned Dorn? Sighing, Kal collapsed.

The tears could not be stopped. Vanaxx helped him up while Sylvara guided him by the shoulder to a nearby chair.

Zalanthas stood at the junction of magickal energies. Invisible to the Dim, these energies weaved in and through creation. They cackled green and golden if a Wizard opened up his third eye to see the world in terms of its primordiality. Where these lines converged, nodes coalesced into spheres. Nonmagickal people saw these places as tranquil glens, serene waterfalls, or majestic clearings. Their hair stood up on the back of their necks when they approached these places. The surrounding area of a node emanated the raw psychic energy of the type of magick it fed. Some were peaceful and good; others were destructive and evil. Sometimes these nodes became warped by the magicks they fueled. Since nodes enhanced a wizard's power, many wars were fought over them. Even now, Allurian nobles gawked enviously at the power Zalanthian mages could command, though they never defiled the Ancestral Wood for the purposes of its power.

Vanaxx motioned Sylvara to the other side of the room. "You were wise to bring him here and seek my counsel. This close to the node will conceal him. He'll be safe here…safe for now," Vanaxx whispered. The powerful presence of those magickal energies radiated a strong field that masked any spell of finding or discovery the Allurians might work to find him. Even now, they might be scrying.

"I'm glad. Does that mean you welcome me?" Sylvara looked concerned.

"The tension between us can wait."

"Father!"

"Enough! We won't discuss this. You've a strange habit of bringing home stray humans. At least this time, perhaps, it is the will of the Goddess Queen, and not a lowborn human husband."

In his wallowing, both knew Kal didn't hear them. An awkward silence stretched between them like the time it took to forge a great sword. Closing his eyes and drawing in a deep breath, Vanaxx let calmness and reason return.

"By the Goddess," he paused. "For now, consider yourself my guest. If you must remain, then remain as companion to this young man. Technically, you're not permitted in this dwelling, but his arrival is unexpected. Like yours. Live with him and watch over him."

He looked down at the young man. "He's been draining his own inner energy to stand and talk here. He's truly spent all of his power. Tear trails shimmered in the twilight-lit library. Staring off into the distance, Kal grew distant and removed as he dreamt of a world where his activism had not cost others their lives. Actions had a price. They always did.

"Through our spy network, we know he fought his brother in dragon-form outside the Eastern Gate several weeks ago. If that's true, they'll be after him. Nobody must know of the prince's station. The Wizardslayers are formidable, even for us. Hide him amongst the survivors of the Vendan massacre and the other Lightdwellers in the human quarter. But make sure the printer understands the sensitivity of hiding the second-born Prince of Alluria."

"Who else knows we met this night?"

"Only archers that escorted us here. They heard everything," Sylvara said. "The elves only saw him as Mage and Lightdweller in our meeting. Nobody outside this room and them knows he is the prince."

Vanaxx turned to his daughter. "Those archers do not say what they think, but by their actions you can tell that your former detail will always protect the House of Quintoriel, even its exiled daughter. They will protect you both." She nodded, her eyes filled with pride. "Take them with you. Have them take the role of lowborn.

Hide them in plain sight." With that, Vanaxx threw a small fortune of gold coin at her feet in a coin purse. She understood. She would hide with him, secure lodging in the city, and the status quo between her and her father would remain, even if she now could dwell within the city walls of Zalanthas. Turning his back to her, he faced away from her.

Regret filling his heart, he spoke over his shoulder. "It's good to have you back in the city nearby." She already left without his knowledge, and his words fell upon dead silence.

Chapter 3

For several weeks, four healers entered a small chamber. They took different eight-hour shifts, and the Prime Magus only used his eldest and most gifted students. They sat chanting in a dark chamber underneath the palace. Torches and candelabra lit. Each wore a black robe, embroidered in the runes of true speech. King Darnashi's mangled body lie naked with some parts of his armor and flesh fused together — molten iron and scorched skin. For weeks, the healers sedated him. The healers tried to separate out the solidified parts of enchanted armor. They layered spell of motionlessness, bone-knitting, flesh-regeneration, and they siphoned the lifeforce of prisoners. At the edge of the room, discarded skulls and bones were scattered all in an effort to save the king. Their very essence drained and made nothing more into the cinder of bone and ash after such spells. The souls and flesh folded into each working, the tendrils of their spirit caught in the magick and folded into each other like the blacksmith's hammer folded steel layers into one blade. The magick ceased for a time like the blacksmith putting the sword once again into water only to return it again to the heat of the forge. The folding of souls and flesh continued.

In his mind, the King Darnashi watched them work. The magick felt cold and hung in the air like charred meat. King Darnashi's astral form separated by his own arts, a will that's magick flooded wildly. Occasionally, Darnashi appeared to his healers. He urged them on. When he appeared, they worked much more efficiently looming as a spectre near death. In that form, he dreamt and thought about his brother. He felt the leash of life and death tugging at him. The magick tether of a silver line bonded soul to body. Caught between two worlds, the passage of time seemed meaningless. His astral-soul yearned to live, and the forces of the Wizardrium needed him desperately. But his brother…his memories returned to that display of power.

Kal evaded a dragon in bird form and with two simple spells of force, Kal succeeded where Darnashi could not, Kalero had played him, egged on his ego, dug his nails into him, and he had done so with calculation and cunning. Somewhere, deep down in the pain, Darnashi smiled. His brother was dangerous, not the whimsical idealistic idiot he thought him to be.

He had calculated and evaded powerful magicks at the tribunal, and who knows how this would have played had Darnashi let the Prime Magus and his agents battle him. Pride. That was his problem. Both of theirs, actually. A family trait, he supposed.

The Prime Magus stood at the tip of the staircase of the chamber. He bore his emerald-ladened staff, and black and gray robes. A fifth robed figure approached. "We are just about done, we think. There's little more we can do."

"You've done good, Nagol. Bring his astral form back into his body and wake him." Bowing, Nagol signaled to the others to end the weeks long spells. Truth be told, the armor-form had saved his life. Parts of the dragon-form seeped into his flesh, leaking valuable magickal energy to fuel and fuse parts of him together in a new way. The lingering essence of the dragon bought him time, time for others to regenerate, transmute, morph, and siphon lifeforce to ground his soul to new composite flesh.

Before him, Darnashi writhed in pain as the four healers used their will to heal his mangled body. Pink clouds of magickal dust and energy washed over the burnt and torn flesh. While the flesh returned, parts of the disenchanted dragon armor proved fruitless to remove, and parts of his leg would never work the same way. Darnashi's cheek and part of the forehead had been seared off revealing parts of the bone and muscle beneath. His eye socket now bore a black gem, which seared with a red glow intermittently as he grew in anger, anguish, and pain. Four tattooed sharp spikes jutted out of the other eye, which preserved its function. But, now, Darnashi could see the auras of magickal energy and lifeforce around every person. In the burnt eye, the only way he could preserve his vision was to convert and combine it with his inner mage eye. The mage eye, or inner eye, is the spiritual lens through which any wizard may view the supernatural energies of the world. He was now permanently open to the magickal and psychic energies of the universe. The same maddening energies stir insanity in the most gifted and calm of wizards, which made this gift used only when necessary in the most powerful of wizards.

The Prime Magus came up next to him. Darnashi's face was contorted in pain. He could speak, but when he did, he clenched his teeth in pain. Neither dared to break the concentration of the healers, especially this close to the end of the spellcasting. Kneeling, the Prime Magus took his Lord's gloved hand and shook his head as if to say "No word yet," then the Prime Magus's eyes softened as if to say, "You are my greatest student."

Darnashi's eyes widened in return. Madness, pain, and a moment of softness filled his eyes. His return gaze said, "Find him. Find him at all costs." The Prime Magus bowed. Darnashi screamed again.

The magickal pink dust settled over his flesh as his skin, bone, sinew, and marrow knitted itself together permanently this time. The Prime Magus had to leave Darnashi that way, ushered away by one of the apprentices. Climbing the stairs to the chamber, he entered an upper hallway of pristine white marble.

From behind, a balding man with strong epicanthic folds of his eyes approached, Commander Tao, regional commander of the Wizardslayers. Two of his lieutenants followed behind. He wore ceremonial armor of a black Hecatium with gold and copper inlay—parts of the same metal that redirects raw magickal energy. In the center, a wyrm encircled a flaming sword, the arcablade. Slung at his hip were a set of swords, the curved arcablade, and the smaller crescent blade. The tanto dagger lay across his back vertically on his belt.

"Sire," Tao bowed, "the patrols have come back. No sign of him."

"And the scryers?" The Prime Magus asked.

"Incapable of finding him," Tao said.

"He must be hiding in a place of power that might mask his aura. One does not use such powerful magick and recover overnight either." The Prime Magus sighed. "Get me all the intelligence we have on his father and mother. We could be missing something."

"Sir," Tao said obediently. He was about to turn when the Prime Magus stopped him.

"Right now, cancel all other active pursuits and investigations," he closed the door behind him softly, his eyes lit by maddening torchlight. "We must find Kalero. Find him. Kill him. He is the most dangerous threat this kingdom has ever faced. Don't stop until he is found."

Tao nodded and answered in stoic silence. The Prime Magus saluted; Tao gestured accordingly and reversed his heels, conferring with his lieutenants.

The Prime Magus climbed another set of stairs to the battlement. Several guards of the Central Keep gave him a wide birth. In the distance, he could see the Mandarian stretch of mountains and forested valley floor. Pine-crowned hills concealed the entire glacial mountains, and a low-lit blue radiated from the moon on a cloudless night. The expanse of stars and night comforted him. Soon, Alluria would rival the power of the stars, and only one could pose a threat. The screams echoed in the halls, and the Prime Magus drew fury from that pain, but also power. He fixated on Kalero, the hapless scholar already a folk hero of the Eastern Gate. His victory was soon becoming legend, and it made the Dims even more emboldened against the Crown. Tomorrow, he would order their death and publically display the minstrels that composed those folk songs, and send the Allurian orchestra to play a beautiful concert in the same square underneath their rotting corpses.

Chapter 4

Facing a mirror just above an open chest, Commander Tao stared at himself with a cold distance. Commander Tao dropped his gauntlets into his chest and plopped his chestplate into the chest. As he stood in front of the mirror, a tightness gripped his throat. He hunted his childhood friend, and before everyone, he never blinked at his orders. How could he? Many regarded him favorably. Anytime a wizard went rogue, traded in black market spells, or posed a threat to the Allurian way of life, he gladly answered the call alongside his units. King Hiraeus and his father went back an entire lifetime, and when it was time to take oath and defend Alluria by defending the Tremayne line, Tao thought their friendship would be like Hiraeus and his father, Wei. Nobody questioned his loyalty. Growing up, Tao was friend to Darnashi as well, but something had gripped him. He was no longer the same.

Neither Dim, but not charmed with the mageborne soul that allowed magick, a Wizardslayer was something in between. A

Flight of the Ravenhawk

Wizardslayer intuited a spell's energy, determined its scope, and reacted instinctively to magick. Once the intuition registered the magick, the Wizardslayer deflected its power, conducting it with the focus of enchanted metal in their armor and weapons. They spent years learning to connect with their weapons and honing their intuitions. This intuition gave them what appeared to be supernatural powers, even though all the powers they had were welded into their armor by enchantment and artifice. They intuited a spell's type and energy, and communed with the mystic metal Hecatium that drained the lifeforce of a mageborne soul. Wizardslayers could channel magickal energies in spells, dissipate it, or redirect it back at their attackers in the dissipated form. Hecatium posed only a threat to mageborne, and so the Allurian failsafe against the dangers of magick was an elite fighting force inside enchanted Hecatium armor.

On his mirror, a photograph pictured him and Kal just two years ago. They smiled with their backs to the new highway of rail lines connecting the West to Alluria—another magicktech marvel of Allurian ingenuity. He snatched it with shaky fingers and sat on the bed facing the opened windows and double doors that led out to his stone patio overlooking the inner courtyard of the palace grounds. That was a good day. The sun shone brilliantly but was tempered by clouds. Men and women, dim, royal, noble— all gathered to see King Hiraeus, Queen Enayra and the brothers dedicate the new technology. The future seemed bright then. Captains of industry and mage lords alike were all optimistic about the new democratized technology.

Never did Tao think his world, his kingdom would be so dysfunctional that he was forced to choose between Alluria and Kalero Tremayne. For him, they were always the same thing, and a fury built up in him. He followed his orders. He did his duty. For Wei and Tao, honor was everything, and pledged to this family and this kingdom, he obeyed. In this room, Tao could show his regrets, but here they were equally buried every morning with new dawn's light that shone in the great windows like ashes carried in the wind over the sea.

Flaring his nostril and exhaling, he rose from the bed, grabbed his arcablade, and decided to loosen the regrets in his heart. On his patio, he focused on the moon in the etched blade. His fingers ran across its edge. With this blade, he was sure. Whenever it dispatched foe, he never hesitated. The sword symbolized a certainty that life completely lacked. That's why he came out here. He danced the martial form of his father's father, and perhaps his father before him. Balanced and graceful, the sword arched in poetic circles of deadly beauty in his hands. Up slice, down slice, slide slice twice—he breathed with every motion, the oxygen circulating his blood almost in step with every motion. In his mind's eye, Tao conjured imaginary enemies, and projected them in front of him. From his hip, he flung the smaller crescent blade, and it sung and moved around him, floating in sync with the flowing circular form of the arcablade. Crescent blade and the arcablade glinted in the moonlight. The martial dance ended with evasion and slice with each attacker.

In minutes, he threw a small towel over his shoulders. The cold night air finally caught him in one shiver as sweat steamed from his body.

"No regrets," he said to himself and the moon before going inside to bed.

Chapter 5

For three days, Kalero slept, and Sylvara watched over him. She had brought him to the Vendan quarter, to the House of Dorn and had her stock of healing herbs, potions, and salves moved here. Several Lightdweller clerics had used the divine energies of their faith, and began recirculating the inner energy Kal had wasted in fury and flight. One heavy-set fellow, Brother Whitakker, a human that everyone called Whiskers, was particularly nosy about the young lad, but Dorn had reassured him. Dorn said he was a scribe, and well learned in the areas of history, metaphysics, and the theories of magick. Though Dim, many teachers – such as these – were common for young noble houses in Alluria. Brother Whittaker came by every day with soup and new bandages.

The Vendan Quarter had long been host to a Lightdweller Temple, a faith as long as Alluria had been a kingdom. For these past five centuries, this temple, like others, housed the scriptures and teachings of the Lightdweller faith. Like the Star worship of the Goddess

Queen, the Lightdwellers preached a philosophy of service and care to the Other that is not oneself as its central claim. The strange irony of the two faiths was that while the Goddess-Queen was less personal than her deification, the Light was more personable to the humans than the metaphors of harmony, unity, and light of the Goddess-Queen. Yet, both were philosophies of peace, and so a few of the Elves in this quarter, mostly lowborn, had joined and maintained the Lightdweller Temple for many centuries and some had been alive in more peaceful times between humans and elves. These elders welcomed the humans into their city. Brother Whittaker had fled persecution of another. Lord Tranek of a minor Noble House on the Western edge of the Allurian Kingdom.

Dorn's darkened skin, and barbed beard hugged Rigela as he entered. He had found work touching up an Elven librarian's own printing press. The work had been the same, remaking some of the letters on the press, finding a new mixture of ink that worked will with the elven vellum, and getting Kal's books into wider circulation to the nearby Kingdoms as ordered by King Vanaxx Quintoriel. In all of this, Dorn was always bitter when he came home. The Librarian's standards and hubris were impossible, and several weeks ago, Isadora, Geru, and Naxon died. The capital city fell into chaos; the Wizardrium taking control of sympathetic and liberal Houses to the inequality of the Dims on the very day he took Rigela to the market leaving Isadora home.

Yet today, of all days, Kal had come. As he promised, he had talked to the King, or so the story had been told. Kal had bested his own brother, who had taken dragon form, as a hawk and spellcaster. He'd first heard it from a trading caravan at a market at the edge of the ancestral forest. He had been sent to pick up a package of parchment. Everyone was singing the song. Only those deemed worthy could be within the halls of Zalanthas. All commerce took place among the many trade routes as it had for the past twenty-four centuries at the edges of the ancestral woods.

Dorn entered the room. Sylvara sat next to him, her eyes never leaving him. "Is he conscious?"

"He stirs, but nothing so far." She anointed his head with enchanted oils.

"I did not know the daughter of the King would be my house guest, and my quarters so lavish. Forgive the untidiness. Rigela and I are just getting used to being…." He could not find the words to talk about his family's death. He swallowed holding back tears. "Being *us*."

Sylvara's purple eyes gave off a sense of calm reassurance. "I find human company most refreshing. The disorder is very welcome from the drab routine of elven tradition."

"Is that so?" said Dorn in utter disbelief. A slight grin parted his face.

Rigela entered, her small frame contrasting against the young elf. She carried a pot of elvish tea. "I really love this elven hibiscus with cinnamon and licorice root. You both should have some. It's been a long few days." She offered four cups considerately to Sylvara, her father, one for Kal if he should awake, and then served herself last. Sylvara took notice of the respect Rigela showed with little understanding of elven ways.

"Thank you," Sylvara said. She did not say anything about the botched steeping of the tea. Humans were not skilled in high elven culture, and she liked the spontaneity of humans. She loved that a human teenager would see nothing wrong with having a morning tea at a non-tea hour. Her husband had been the same way. That is the way of humans. They were spontaneous because they did not bake in the habits of centuries. They were brash, quick to act, and sometimes reckless according to stern elven judgment, yet that's also what made them strong in Sylvara's eyes. While elves depended on what worked for centuries, they were slow to adapt and change whereas the humans could be enticingly pragmatic and spontaneous.

She waved the tea in Kal's direction, and he stirred. Immediately, she put the tea down. Rigela and Dorn watched in silence.

"Where am I?" he barely got out, the words stumbling to the surface.

"In my house," Dorn reassured. Kal opened his eyes. He saw young Rigela and Dorn. He smiled. "I think you've met, but all the same, this is Sylvara. She's to stay here as well, sorta watch out for you and us." Kal took this information in, and looked back at Dorn.

"Zalanthas?"

"Yes, sire." Dorn nodded to Rigela, and they both bowed. Sylvara looked curiously at them.

Kal pushed himself up somewhat, struggling against fatigue. His arms twitched as he raised himself to sit up. "There will be none of that while I am here."

"I'm to hide here for some time, and not be a prince." He motioned for them to rise. "This is your house, not mine. Your sanctuary."

"You're still my prince, ma'lord." Rigela nodded at Dorn's words.

"Then consider it an order from your prince to humble yourself before whatever cover I've been given." They both nodded in agreement.

Sylvara looked at him. "You're to be a scribe, a former lowborn tutor to one of the Allurian houses. For now, you're to help Dorn at the Zalanthas Library, a short-term work assignment putting some of that scholarly knowledge to use." She looked to hand him her cup of tea.

He sipped it slowly and took a deep breath. Placing his right arm over his eyes, Kal sighed. "The Wizardslayers will come. No matter where I am." He bit his lip, and thought about what might happen to Dorn and Rigela.

"Do I have a name?"

"Ellex Sablon. And perhaps they will come, perhaps not." Sylvara said. "You're in the heart of the new human quarter, right next to the ley lines that intersect in the very heart of the node."

Kal chuckled and exhaled a sigh of relief. A node was a collection of ley lines, energy flows of magick, and only a few sacred places existed in all of creation as intense. The overflowing magick should mask any wizard so the Allurian scryers might never find him. Somehow, he felt his mother's hand in this wisdom to come here, or was it the tingling sense of destiny that made his neck hair stand on end. He needed to figure out his next move.

"I'd ask all of you if I may take my leave of you and return to sleep."

"Yes, ma'lord." Dorn said. Rigela curtsied

Sylvara shot them a disapproving glance. "The two of you will give us away. This is Ellex." Dorn had to look at Rigela. They agreed right then and there, never again.

"Won't he give us away? We're not the only Vendans here," Rigela said.

Kal put his arm down. "Trust me, I will wear a glamour so flawlessly mundane that nobody except you three will see me for who I really am." Beside him, he pointed at Sylvara. "Won't the daughter of a King draw attention to us already in this neighborhood."

Sylvara looked down ashamed. "I am an exile, an outcast, and so to live with humans is…" She paused looking for the right word. "An honor." Kal grimaced. He knew what she meant, and would not ask of her transgression. "Besides, at least, I am now in the city, not a herb witch living in a hut."

As she rose to leave Kal's side, Kal grabbed her hand, and held up his other hand for Dorn and Rigela to stop. "On this day, I pledge to you, to all of you. I will stop my brother. I will return to the throne and take it from him. Alluria will know peace with Zalanthas. And Zalanthas will know a friend in me." He put his head back down. Sylvara, Dorn, and Rigela exchanged glances unsure what to say to each other, so they departed in silence, hope, hanging on the young prince's vow.

****

The Prime Magus paced back and forth. He burned yet another report from the Southeast. Had the Prince gotten lucky? Maybe he still was a ravenhawk incapable of changing back? A wishful thought. A knock wrapped upon his chamber door. He waved his hand and the door flew open. Bowing before crossing the threshold, Tao entered carrying several scrolls sealed in red wax. "I come with the background reports you requested, sire."

"Put them on the desk in my study," the Prime Magus returned.

Saying nothing, Tao did his bidding. When he came out, the Prime Magus motioned for him to leave.

No conventional or magickal means was forthcoming in finding Prince Kalero. For years, the Prime Magus did not want to barter or trade secrets with powers best left to the other spiritual planes. Very few, if any, could converse with those planes, summon the very beings that had seamless knowledge of this corporeal realm, and nobody knew the price such a being of the Underdark would demand. Yet, every solution to the prince's absence seemed to head down this road.

In fact, in more ancient times, the contact with them was more frequent. Such frequent encounters led to religious wars, the corrupting influence of the Underdark, and the rise of the necromantic arts. To allay the rise of these arts and the dangers they posed to civilization itself, a conclave of wizards came together forming the Wizardrium, and the Wizardrium had created the rules of magick in the Allurian Empire to stamp out all knowledge of these spiritual realities—except to those elite few that could control this power—controlling curriculum, monitoring ideas, and ensuring that every copy of these spells and stories of the

Underdark and Overlight remained hidden. When the Wizardrium decided it was best to purge this knowledge, it had only one real obstacle to the creation of a new social order that would promote a naturalized conception of the universe, a vision that ensured no supernatural explanation of magick; the Lightdwellers had a religion that went contrary to this narrative, and it still persisted. Thus, for some time, the Wizardrium dominated and eradicated their presence whenever convenient. As such, the Wizardrium thought to win over the hearts and minds of those learning magick, and secured magick-users and the Wizardrium itself a place of continued power by at first denouncing necromancy and planar magicks, then later by rewriting the history of magickal metaphysics. That's how the Allurian Houses of Nobility and the throne had been formed. Only the truly Enlightened and worthy masters ruled Alluria. These institutions were forged in the fire of protecting all of creation against that which they did not need, nor ever wanted to know.

King Darnashi had not sent for the Prime Magus yet. He still healed. The metal had fused to his flesh, and his one eye was constantly open to the energy of creation itself. The Prime Magus was running out of options, and he bit his lip. Opening oneself up to those energies took its price on a man's soul, let alone his body, and yet it had been the only way to save him. It might be the only way to know Kal's whereabouts. Several powerful apprentices of the Wizardrium's Inner Council had been sent over, employing the necromantic arts to fuse enchanted armor and flesh. There had been no other way. Rubbing his beard, the Prime Magus had to figure out something—some way to find Kalero.

In Alluria to have the King's ear is to wield influence and power, and the Prime Magus had to be both politically cunning and powerful in the High Arts of Magick. To lose the King's ear was also to falter, to be dismissed, and there had been several Prime Magi in the past centuries that were ineffective, selected out of the ranks of the Wizardrium and the Academy of Magery as nothing more than a figurehead for the lower and more ambitious wizards of minor Allurian Houses. The Prime Magus vowed to not be one that let Alluria and all of its glory fall to the hands of such petty conflict.

The Prime Magus called in his servants after sleeping for several hours. "I need liquid silver." His secretary, a dim scribe, wrote down the request in a brash manner. The Prime Magus never bothered to learn his name, Chardon, and never gave him a second thought. He was wiry in build with tall cheekbones that stretched into an elongated face, and he wore a green tunic and simple leggings.

Chardon was about to leave. "That's not all. I will need ten gold coins. I'll also need a body. I tell you this now so that when I am ready, you may keep your ear to the ground. Do not make this an official request. The discretion of this request reflects the office you serve and the life you've given to me. You may have to find someone we can kill. Maybe one of those minstrel fellows. It's clear, however, that it can't be me." The Prime Magus pointed down to a scroll etched in red ink on dark parchment and scroll. "The ritual forbids me to kill the subject. I may need you to do it, Chardon."

Chardon felt the pit of his stomach drop and dare not say no. The Master finally knew his name. He had gotten it right on the first try, and now he was being entrusted with a secret, a dark secret, and a necromantic secret perhaps. Glee filled his heart. All the things done in the Prime Magus's name, finally, he was known to him— the most powerful house and Magelord in the Allurian Kingdom. He nodded in agreement, almost too eagerly the Prime Magus noticed. The Prime Magus tossed him his ring. He caught it in both hands, cupping it as if it were holy wine. The ring bore the seal of the Prime Magus's office, and with it, the enchantments would declare true that Chardon of Mayvana's Hollow served the highest mage in the land.

"Don't just stand there. Off you go!" the Prime Magus bellowed.

On the first day, Chardon requisitioned the ritual components of liquid silver. A lingering sense of power and will could be detected despite lacking his own wizard's eye. Overtaken with determination and concentration, the Prime Magus barely noticed him. Chardon departed, trying to be indispensable to the goals of his master. Rumor had it that the Prime Magus had to be one of the most powerful wizards in all of Alluria.

Chardon spent the next two days talking to menders, mages who specialize in healing and mending matter. He went to their stores and clinics. The Academy of Magery often tried to secure cadavers for the natural study of physiology, and so a request for a nearly-dying man or a corpse was not uncommon. Chardon claimed to come from the Academy, representing them and the interests of the Prime Magus. As an agent of the Wizardrium – insofar as he carried the Prime Magus's ring at the very least –

Chardon also inquired if any of the minstrels remained alive. "The Wizardrium has questions. Any of them will do. I only need one." There was one, a Mrs. Bogarty. Chardon walked down the prison hallway past low-lives and thieves. At the end, a ragged woman in a faded blouse and dirt-stained skirt was roped to the wall. Her hands bore scars of the rope on her wrists, and she ached having been forced to sleep in ridiculous positions. Her skin was a pure white, contrasting against the vile wretched gray stones and black chains barely visible in perpetual torchlight.

"This be the one," the guard said.

"Good," Chardon said. He circled his index finger in the air to the group of guards that escorted him. Instantly, they took a knife out and cut the rope attached to the wall. She tried to bolt, but the guard grabbed her, tossing her over his shoulder as she kicked and screamed. She did no damage to the armor he wore, and Chardon smiled devilishly. He would please his master.

The carriage took all day to circle the city. Chardon could not enter the Wizardrium Grounds until the guard rotation. He paid the guard for his silence. Unconscious, the guard carried the woman's body slung over his shoulder when they departed the carriage.

Through twisting and winding corridors of pink marble they walked. The windows were cut with tiny slits and dark oaken geometric patterns blocked the cold of night. Robed figures wandered the hall, and for an instant, the guard's face trembled. He did not like being this close to the seat of power. Instead, Chardon had truly been on business for the Prime Magus, and guard would not say a thing about delivering this young girl. They walked toward a large obsidian door, behind it: the Prime Magus's chambers, laboratory, and private residence. The guard's legs shook.

Concealing a bitter smile of pride, Chardon snickered. He raised his hand and ring. The ring radiated a spell of recognition. Large circular gears in the oaken design and clockwork mechanism could be heard inside the marbled walls. Huge counterweights heaved and fell. A mixture of enchantment and clockwork engineering chimed, whistled, bellowed and clanged together. This door recognized Chardon's ring, and the request made of its bearer. The door whispered, "Enter" in a soft hissing sound. That was it. The guard ran almost dropping the girl. Chardon caught her unconscious body by wrapping his hands in her tattered dress. She muttered something.

Flight of the Ravenhawk

The Prime Magus stood just inside the door with his hands at his hips. "Ahh. Good. She will do nicely." A long black robe secured by a simple blood red cincture gave definition to his thin build and tall stature. His eyes were almost purely white. The windows had been sealed shut, light-tight. Candlelight and torch light danced and light baubles, the simplest of enchantments, hung in the air. They floated silently, and a cold wind brushed Chardon's hair and several candles strewn about the room. "Follow," the Prime Magus ordered.

Chardon remained silent. He dared not speak since the smell of incense and magical concoctions brewing indicated preparations were already underway, if not finished. The Prime Magus had a look in his eye. It was the look of a man of power and determination. One could feel the very power of his will, even if Chardon failed to be mageborne. With the female in tow, Chardon followed the Prime Magus until they reached a stone altar; it appeared ancient-made of the dolerite bluestone of previous ages when magick openly combined belief in gods of the Underdark and Overlight. Around the blue stone slab, a silver ensorcelled ring encircled the altar. Carved into each eighth segment, a rune glowed red.

Chardon put the woman down. Waving his hand over her head, the Prime Magus awakened the woman, yet she did not have the power to speak, but her eyes screamed. The look of absolute horror filled her mind as she rotated her head. A gag in her mouth kept her screams contained.

"Approach the circle," the Prime Magus said, handing Chardon a dagger, "And slit her throat."

Chardon's hands shook. The Prime Magus could see this as a problem. "Kill her, or I'll kill you." Chardon turned his eyes to the woman fastened to the altar. She shook her head in desperation. But Chardon feared the Prime Magus's power. As Chardon approached her, a tiny pinprick of purple and pink energy tore open a vortex above them. Some *power*, some *thing* wanted these energies in this space. The smell of lingering death and hollowed screams of distant phantasms and other creatures of the Underdark circled above. He did what he was told, and the woman's blood spilled. The blood came down in a gush of crimson. The silver circle radiated an intense red. Chardon could feel the intensity, the power, and did not know it.

Chardon looked down at the woman, her lifeless body fueling something he could not understand. Then, out of his stomach, a serrated sword jutted; he could feel the loss of life and purpose. A slight twinge of his eyebrows signaled his consciousness, his soul being pulled upwards somewhere. He willed himself to hold onto anything, but even as Chardon formed his bodily intentions, his body did not listen like a child who could not fathom the dangers of playing in a storm. It could not listen. His body loomed below. Before him, he saw the vortex, the swirling eddies of magickal ebb and flow between planar realities. Voices of tormented souls sung like sirens, their fiendish wailing beckoning the ensouled ships of the newly deceased.

The Prime Magus had to kill a murderer. Chardon was expendable, and the recently deceased woman's body would be vessel for the ally and powers beyond. The ally beyond had healed King Darnashi. Yet, the Prime Magus cautioned these spellcastings. For the power beyond was nameless, and when a mage casted his will, he spoke a language that committed him to truth. The Prime Magus's words named the true name of summoning: *Elonnel*—the name meant "that which bore witness to all." This magickal language consisted of two parts: a language of true names of all things, and the language of changing. The next word the Prime Magus spoke was, "Jajek tonnu," which meant "come hither." Only by uniting these two languages with the third component of Will could magick technically be done, and so a purple and pink strand left the swirling massive portal above. *Witness come hither*. The magick tasted like raw need, something dark and primal. For many centuries, the mageborne argued if the powers beyond had names, and most regarded the nameless dark as a place of power that only sought the void of being itself. *Elonnel* had a name. A name that directed it to be here, to come when summoned. If Being is life, and certainly there was no word for all of Being, then perhaps the same would be true for the nameless dark. In the magickal language, there was no word for "being" or "totality."

The powers beyond consumed Chardon's soul, and the energies levitated his body leaving no trace of his corpse, only the dead woman remained. Between the purple vortex and the woman, the thread of purple and pink energy connected the heart with the power beyond, and the woman's body came to life. The Prime Magus could feel a sense of satisfaction and peace from whatever it was that entered and circled above. The woman's body moved about, the eyes black, touching the stone and making tactile contact with every surface. It smelled the blood, tasting it off the altar, and faced the Prime Magus. A radiant light of blue energy sparkled as the woman, reanimated by a dark force, saw the silver runic circle below.

"You've built defenses, mage." It tested the integrity of the forged silver ring. The reanimated corpse ran its fingers along the spatial edge of the ring. Sparks flung from its touch. "Smart."

"What do I call you?" the Prime Magus asked.

"Call me Witness."

"Witness, I need to find Kalero Tremayne."

The creature smiled. "To need help from us, you must be desperate Prime one."

"To lose the brother may put a stop to my plans," the Prime Magus said. "Yet, Kalero evades us. Somehow, he is hidden so that no scryer, no location spell, nothing can find him. Even the power of the brotherly connection cannot make it easier. We're at a loss."

"While my connection is between worlds, I may get the answer you wish to know," Witness said. The woman walked back and forth still checking the runic circle. "My price is freedom in the corporeal world."

"A power such as yours cannot be made free."

"Yet, you barter for something you do not know, Prime One."

"Are we bartering?" the Prime Magus spoke a few words, and the blue energy of the shield shot a bolt of lightning at the creature, knocking it back against the altar. Witness's head cocked to the right side. Black eyes stared into oblivion past the Prime Magus.

"Bind me, then. Let me do your will, let me secure the peace of your kingdom lest a war of brother tear asunder the peace you Allurians have tried to build."

"A war?"

"Oh yes, a war. Even now, it is given to me to know that a war unlike any other may enrapture your world. Kal must be stopped. My freedom is that price."

"Bounded freedom? A contradiction in terms," the Prime Magus said. He waved his hand at the possibility. Clearly, the creature knew something, yet to bargain with demons... He sighed. King Darnashi's wishes will be done. The will of the King was the will of the Prime One. They were in unison.

Witness shrugged. "You must understand. Corporeal existence is a freedom from being pure spirit even if it's in the service of a master like yourself. Even now, the smell of blood is a memory I can cherish. We take these memories with us." Witness tasted the blood again on one finger. The psychic resonance of pain and fear fed her. "Choice is yours, mage." Undoubtedly, the Prime One needed Kalero dead. There would be strings attached to this freedom, the nameless dark had its own agenda.

The Prime Magus extended his will in the language of magick, and Witness's eyes widened in shock. The price may come high, but Witness would get out. Witness would be bound, but out, out in the world of elf, dwarf, and man. Witness subdued his will and he could not hear the song of the powers beyond anymore. A mage binding like this required Witness to lower his will to the Prime Magus's spell. He opened his own mind to the Prime Magus, and the power the Prime Magus commanded thundered in his very soul.

The Prime Magus spoke the language of magick. "I bind you, Witness. I bind you to my service, my ambitions, and my goals. I bind you to loyally serve me and securing my safety. I bind you to the task of killing Kalero and seeking him out. You are bound from never taking the life of any other Allurian except Kalero Tremayne. The seal of citizenship will shield all. I bind you to never reveal your nature to anyone lest I will it so."

"Name the ambition that ties me to your will," Witness said.

"The survival of Alluria against all odds, the empire we've built and that King Darnashi's reign will be known forever."

At the word, forever, Witness smiled. Responding back in the language of true magick, Witness spoke. "The pact is made. The deal is done."

Shocked, the Prime Magus saw a piece of parchment float before him inside the ensorcelled circle and vanish in flame. He understood, but too late. Binding was not a binding of the will as much as a mutual spellcasting. Witness had made a deal with him inside the spell binding him, and he had asked the ambition, the ambition that King Darnashi's reign be known "forever." He had no idea how Witness would interpret it, but it was clear that they were at an impasse. With the binding done, the runic circle dropped, and Witness was free.

"He's in Zalanthas, next to their node of power. It's been shielding him for these past few weeks as you search in vain." In a flash, the Prime Magus was gone. He travelled in the secret ways that wizards do when haste must be made. Like sand collecting together, he came next to his beloved student and King. In the throne room, several advisors were going over the airship rotations Alluria's skyfleet as he appeared. Darnashi looked at him stunned, and he quickly dismissed the advisors.

"Zalanthas."

"Send the slayers, immediately. A small force, not large. Above the clouds, I think. Kill him. Bring me his head," Darnashi smiled. These words came together, almost incoherently as his smile interrupted. "In and out quickly, so the elves don't know we were there…if we can help it." Kal would certainly die.

When the Prime Magus returned to his tower, Witness, hugging the blood-stained sword, lay asleep. Etched in its face, a smile parted its lips. Despite the binding, Alluria would not be torn asunder in the prophetic war. In the Prime Magus's haste, the portal was still open, left open, and the runic protections were gone; the Prime Magus wondered what this mistake would cost him. He closed it with a word, and fell over from exhaustion. What had he done?

Chapter 6

During the last two weeks, Kalero fell into a routine. As Ellex the scribe, he had been involved in printing a large number of books. The Librarian acted as both archivist and publisher. Every text published and written could be mailed and then catalogued in the Zalanthas library. Many of the texts coming into the Elven lands were surprisingly abundant. He cataloged works on plant sciences, agriculture, the metaphysics of magick, various ancient religions, and some more contemporary works on Lightdweller theology, even his own book. The library made some more funds in the commerce between the races by printing some of his books on order from nearby kingdoms. The Librarian had a long face, and very hawkish features. He seemed disapproving of Dorn's press operating skills. "The human does not strive towards perfection, but only the function of printing," he complained to Kalero. "A man should seek perfection in his art."

The librarian had a name, but nobody knew it. He only answered to the title and vocation of his life's work. "Librarian," someone called, and he would get off his stool in the middle desk that oversaw all four massive wings jutting out in each cardinal direction. He would walk anyone to what they wanted without need of looking in the massive card catalog behind him. He may also be the only elf in the entire ancestral realm that could also openly scoff at the ignorance of minor lords and children of the highborn. He had lived for fourteen centuries; he walked everywhere in the great library, and knew every shelf inside and out. In fact, rumors abounded that he had invented the same cataloging system that all races used. His assistants knew that as long as he lived they would never be in charge, so they demonstrated immense patience with the Librarian's impatience.

One day, when Kal was sorting through some documents, he came upon a magickal scroll, a list of spells of how to transmute plant life. It was written in the language of making and changing, from the Dwarven Spellmaster of Vinchento, three centuries ago, if memory served him correctly. Kal sighed, brushing his hand on the native craft language of magick. Dorn had snuck him some books on calling and summoning, and Kal checked these texts against the historic Scriptures of Light at the heart of Lightdweller theology. The Librarian came up behind him. He cocked an eyebrow as Kal read over a very difficult spell to transmute oak.

"Too much power that one is," he explained. "Oaks in the ancestral realm are older than the civilizations around them. You understand that tongue, lad?"

Kal took a long breath. "No, of course not." Kal left it there and walked away. He regretted the altercation with his brother, and this conflict weighed heavily on his heart. He had permanently scarred his brother. Then again, he'd given him a chance—a chance to honor their parents, and far removed from the realities of politics, something in his brother had changed. Kalero should have noticed. Nash had used a shapeshifting spell of dark magic. Somehow, the armor he wore had the life essence of a dragon morphed into it, giving him instantaneous access to that form. He either was in league with someone who gave him that suit, or studied those powers and made it himself. Either way, Darnashi had been corrupted by necromantic arts and employed those arts in that last fight.

Even amidst the turmoil of his own heart, Kal's work as a scholar and archivist was impeccable, and the Librarian seemed to test him. Ellex, as he was called, did not notice, but carried on with his duties barely noticing what the Librarian said; he seemed to register it and take to the library like no human ever had. On one occasion, the Librarian asked him to translate a phrase a visiting scholar had wanted. Without thought, Kal merely wrote it down and returned to his archiving of returned scrolls and books. On another occasion, Kal had located several scrolls intuitively to a visiting elven wizard from the Wayfaring Kingdom. Kal had been so naïve, so lost in his ivory tower to notice how far his brother had gone that he didn't notice that the Librarian spoke in high Elven. "I suppose Vinchento's spell of transmutation should be catalogued as an example of Mindorian enchantments."

Kalero thought about it. "No, the Mindorus enchantments have a strictly military application and precede Vinchento by about two centuries." These words came from a lifetime of scholarly reflex. Kal bit his lip and closed his eyes, scolding himself internally.

"I don't suppose," Kal said, "you could forget hearing what I just said." Kal opened one eye. He hadn't realized that the Librarian had gotten close to him on a stool. The Librarian's knobby nose held light wire frames that encircled his judgmental eyes.

"You're not as you seem, are you Ellex Sablon?"

"I've given word enough to be silent about that question," Kal said. He turned away, trying to ignore him.

"Yet, you read the language of making and changing," the Librarian said, "A feat not too common for any of us. A certain soul is what you need. A gift to see and do what others cannot."

Kal bit his lip. "I miss it, Master Librarian. Now, I'm here. That's all I can say to you. I do not take you as a fool, or one to be fooled. These are vows I have taken to the highest office in your land."

"No doubt, also the reason why you've taken residence with Dorn and the King's daughter, Sylvara, under the same roof." The Librarian, then, looked next to what Dorn had been printing. *Confessions of a Theistic Wizard* had been ordered to the Southeast, and several underground temples of the Lightdwellers had been hosting reading groups on this book. The King also seemed interested in circulating such a book, an indirect way to strike back at the ruling ideologies of the Allurian Empire. Its central premise was that wizardry should be in the service of others, and such a conception of magick, though heretical to Allurian society and all it stood for, was, in fact, rooted in Lightdweller theology that united both Clerics and Wizards to work for the betterment of all creation. With the establishment of the Wizardrium, the Allurians had tried to cleanse their academies of these movements long ago, even so much as calling for an inquisition on those academicians that thought differently.

"Hmm...a deduction from the evidence might be that you're Kalero Tremayne, wizarding prince and heretic of the Allurian Empire."

Kal tried to keep his temper.

"Bah, you're too thin for a prince," the Librarian grabbed his hands and turn them over. He examined the palms intently. "Hands have never known a hard day's work, though." Kal grabbed back his hands.

"Enough, Librarian!" Kal commanded. "I told you. I have given my word."

"In annoyance, young prince, you give yourself away." Suddenly, Kal knew the elf had played him, annoying him, getting in his space, to see if he both knew Elven enough to employ conjugations associated with nobility, as any young Allurian Prince may know from tutelage, and to quiz him on the parchment he read. Putting two and two together, the Librarian had confirmed his suspicions after these long weeks. Kal, though even tempered and more down to earth than, perhaps, any Allurian prince before him was, to his own dismay, still a prince. "I apologize." The words seemed foreign to him.

"Tensions are high between our nations," the Librarian squawked, "Your presence will be discovered. One way or the other. Such secrets can't be kept for long."

"And may I ask: Will you keep this secret? It is your King's will."

Over his glasses, the Librarian glared scornfully. "My will is always the will of the king. It has been so for fourteen centuries and will be as long as I draw breath. Since you are new here, I can only surmise you are ignorant of this fact." He paused. "Your secret is safe with me."

"I don't know how to stop my brother. Short of killing him." Turning in his stool at his desk, Kal lifted a leather satchel that hid several commentaries on necromantic arts.

"Death may be your only way." The Librarian appeared human for the first time. His eyes softened. "Now that that's cleared up. How might this elf further the aims of peace?"

"When I fought my brother, he had imbued the essence of a dragon into his armor. That means necromantic arts, powerful ones. They'd have to have a place, a place where they did that to living creatures. Dragons no less. I don't know what powers my brother has, or if it is even him, but I need ways to stop necromantic energy."

"That's why Dorn has been sneaking you calling and summoning texts. Summoning arts are a tricky business."

"Yes, a price is always paid for such transactions with the Underdark. I've been wondering if there is an analogue, a way to call on the powers of the Overlight in Lightdweller theology. The thought is for every dark power there's a light counterweight to restore balance."

"Let's assume this premise governs creation. It's the very sound premise. And shall I dare say a common belief in many of the native religions to both Dwarves, and the Elven worship of the Goddess-Queen."

Kalero nodded. "I don't want to kill what I swore to love."

The Librarian said nothing, but hopped off his stool. Grabbing his small cane, the Librarian hobbled up the stairs in direction to the section on magickal spells. He motioned for the young man to follow. Several of the assistants passed them. Some eyed them both curiously, but soon looked away when the Librarian seemed normal again in his irritable sounding voice. "Come Ellex. Let's get to that cataloging project for the King," he barked in Elven.

For the next few days, the Librarian was unusually preoccupied with a research project. The Librarian was a natural ally to the young wizard. The Librarian gathered several old texts, some from the past five centuries. Soon, Kal learned of the order and union between cleric and wizard, the very history the Allurian libraries had abandoned and purposefully pushed out of memory. It had been such a common pairing a thousand years ago. Indeed, even the Lightdweller temples had been more plentiful in earlier centuries, and accounts of the Wizardrium's cultural war against them was well documented in Elven. Only a scattering of this history survived in Vendan libraries. Blacklisted texts were hard to come by. Kal knew there were gaps, but not this extensive.

"In Alluria, these histories are censored."

"Indeed," the Librarian muttered. "Those who hold power over others control information. It is the same everywhere. All are guilty of excluding some, taking advantage of ignorance for personal gain, and that's why Librarians of my order swear against the withholding of information."

Lowering his face to his book, Kal returned to his reading. The Librarian admired his concentration. Some elven wizards could not muster that much concentration, and he soon learned that Kal had a mastery of the wizard's tongue, elven (both high and low), and basic Dwarven. As second-born, the boy had been quite content not to hold the reigns of power. Many of the second-born, even amongst the elves, are happier than those that take up the mantle of obligation. Elven literature provided many examples.

****

Kal's dreams lingered on the tensions and anxieties in his heart. These anxieties weighed his heart down and prevented a good sleep.

A soft summer light shot through the window. He dressed in his simple outdoor leggings, bore staff in his right hand, and draped his satchel on his shoulder. He prepared a few wards about his person in case Sylvara wandered a distance from the node at the center of Zalanthas. The magick held tight and fast around him. It felt like a heavy coat of fur, and to his surprise, he could not be more wrong about the distance. They never left Zalanthas.

Eventually, Sylvara came his way; she bade him to follow her deeper into the Ancestral Wood. She glided in the forest, her footfalls making no sound. As the morning light shown true her white dress changed from blue to its pure white. Cascading golden-lit sun beams cut through the emerald canopy. Closer and closer, Kal could feel the pulse of life and energy as they approached the ancient site. The pulse of life beat in the heart of whatever they approached. "Follow the harmony, Kalero Tremayne," Sylvara said. "Feel its intensity, its allure, its ambiance." Her eyes danced in the rays of light that parted the golden and green leaves above. She had pulled back her hair, and she skimmed the tall forest floor's tall grass with her fingertips. Each blade tickled her palms, and Kalero, now, understood. Extending his perception, he opened his magickal eye to the world and saw the glowing intensity of a river of gold lifeforce, the light heavy as moss and the river as viscous as sap. The magick of this place seeped and bubbled like the rich magma of sullen earth. It pulsed and resonated all around him, an orchestra of harmonious energies ebbing and flowing with life itself. They continued to walk.

When the forest parted, they came upon a glen; a waterfall cascaded down to a small pool on the other side. Beams of light fell upon the pool and rippled out in circlets of yellow that faded back into the pool of water. "Enter the pool," Sylvara said, "and just listen. Listen to nature itself. Stop thinking with the concepts you use to understand the world, and just listen."

Turning away from Sylvara, Kal dropped his satchel and staff on the bank. Unsure, he turned back, but Sylvara was nowhere. She had merely brought him; she wanted to show him what he must learn to do. He rolled up the end of his leggings. Instantly, a sense of calmness and tranquility permeated his very being as he took his first steps into the pool. All thoughts went away, the ceaseless motion of consciousness becoming the stillness of the pool's reflection. He found the calmness in silence similar to the meditative practice he used to hold the form of ravenhawk as he flew from the clutches of his brother, yet there was a substantial difference too.

This warming sensation, he thought came from his feet instead, came from elsewhere—not without, but within. That wasn't quite right—not within, but without. Not that either. Both in and out, these feelings entered and left, leaving him cold and warm, shuttering and steady, part and whole, and one and all. The forest taught him to listen: root and branch, hole and tree.

A dull ring in his ears shut out the forest noise, and he touched the sun's rays with an outstretched hand. He could hear the light at that point; it announced itself as kayaj in the language of true names. When the wind blew through the trees, he could hear the true speech of creation, whispers of elms, saplings, oaks, and birches. In his mind, each name came to him. With those names, his very intuition opened up receiving creation's gift, the true name. On his feet, he could feel the word for silt and sediment. The plunking noise of water sounded with the term toka. The buzzing wings of a nearby humming bird carried the true name of itself in the very flutter of its wings. Finally, he understood. If he wanted to hear the very source of balance he strove to understand, then he must open his intuition, his heart and his very being to what was known in silence, in the unfolding presence, than in thought of the thing itself.

"You must empty yourself in order to fill yourself," Sylvara sat on the bank, appearing as if she had never left. Looking at Kal, she saw his eyes widen. His lips almost mouthed how, but she spoke over him. "These ambient energies are an excess and call out to wizard and cleric. Each in different ways," she folded her hands to the center of her chest. "You can root yourself and absorb these energies."

"But first, I must listen to them," Kal returned. She nodded yes, and left him in silence. She dove in, and communed in her own elven way with the sacred space she shared.

On the next day, Kal came alone early in the morning. He found the glen by listening to the forest. He came to the bank, sat cross-legged, and placed his staff flat over his knees. Taking in a resting breath, he opened his wizard eye again, and let his entire being join the saturated energies of this sacred space. The currents and eddies of magickal force flowed around and through him. He now knew why the elves guarded their node, where forest, earth, light, and life come together. The entire race, if not corrupted, could hear what he needed to draw from. The energies poured forth into his being. Had Kal opened his eyes, he would have known on this day that he glowed with an intense golden aura. He tapped into the reservoirs of being, could feel the trees, and followed the roots. He found the root, the very root of being itself, and understood the forest not as space filled with separate entities, but an amorphous and organically unfolding entity. I am all, and all is I. Creation is always in motion, always unfolding, always relating, and only for a short time coming together in loose forms. The magickal language of changing and making manipulated what loosely came together, but there may be a deeper magick apprehended in the very being of the Source's song.

When Kal emerged, he found himself beaming, feeling every part of the whole, but could not keep this insight for long. Soon, the distractions of the scholarly Wizard mind intruded back into him. At last, he understood. Only with disciplined practice could he listen to the Light, to the ever-unfolding divine nature at the heart of every being's name. The true name allowed a way to access this totality, this harmony, but insofar as one's heart could not sustain that awareness of the whole, evil would seep into the heart, and abuse the the true name. Evil wizards trapped Being and abused Creation at the expense of the very harmony evident to those who can listen to creation's call.

By listening to creation's call, Kal visited the glade many times over the next few days. These ambient energies were easily absorbed, and by charging himself, he could store those reservoirs of energy, not defile this sacred space, and empower himself with the added benefit of the very mana this space produced. At night, he casted light baubles, shedding light on the ancient scriptures he and the Librarian went through. He discovered ways to counter his brother's necromantic power. He found a few counter spells; some ways to deflect those energies, but no spell could dispel the positive from the negative. Despite all his research, one must embrace the negativity of life.

In those lonely nights, Sylvara watched him from afar, shrouded in the leaves and growths of the ancient woods. In the treetops, she ordered her retinue to back off from watching him. They kept their distance, and never let their presence be known, but retreated back to a safe perimeter. The lonely human had more concentration in his heart and purpose than she had ever known in an elf. His purposefulness was almost elven, and she found it alluring, even beautiful. In fact, his obsession and directed purpose was almost too elven. She would lean on those trees, and the forest would catch her as she walked. She listened to creation in her own way as a druid and conduit of these energies herself. As the forest's guardian, she felt Kal's sense of balance and life like a cook knowing the secret ingredient by mere smell.

He stood up and looked in the trees. "Sylvara, come down," he said dryly without looking up from his books and scrolls. "Come down and keep me company."

"How did you know I was there?"

"You'll be mad if I tell you." A loud thump sounded as he closed his tome. "Then again, maybe you won't be."

"Tell me." She jumped down from the solid oak across from him.

"Feeling, I think."

"What?"

"I can't see you or detect you in the forest." He gestured to the whole forest with both arms. "This place knows you as its protector, its guardian. It hides you from the sight of wizarding eyes. No locating spell will find you here in this forest, so I looked where spells could not know things. There, I found your silhouette in the trees above."

"There's more behind those eyes," she said laughing. "A spell to find where no spell can be."

"And, your father and King gave me shelter. I don't know why, but my importance might mean you're close. A fact I've had faith in these past few nights. Kings and lords move people around like chess pieces. Always calculating. I'm not yet certain why I am permitted sanctuary. And, I had a sense you were near. I could almost feel it."

"In the tree song, the wind and leaves sing together," she exclaimed with excitement. Kal nodded a silent yes, and she could not believe it. Like her, Kal was starting to hear the tree song, the very power and emanation of balance and life at the heart of the Ancestral Wood. If the tree song told him she was near, certainly, she must trust him now more than ever.

"He could not know for sure. Destiny is a funny thing, but my father has lived long enough to see patterns, feel and hear them, perhaps like the tree song. Elves live a long time and are very calculating, but sometimes we guess," Sylvara said. She turned to him sincerely resting her head on one hand. "So are human princes and kings, guessers and calculators?" she asked.

Kal shrugged. His silence saying more than he could on the subject.

"My father sees goodness in you Kalero Tremayne. He's impressed, not too many humans can do that." The light bauble bounced away from his shoulder as she lowered herself beside him.

Kal put both hands under his head. "Why does he not send for you?" Kal asked. "People treat you with a deference, but not the same respect as when his name is mentioned."

"You've heard the whispers," she returned his gaze with eyes fragile and stoic.

Kal nodded again.

"Thirty years ago, I married without permission. I married a merchant, a human. Malex. While my father would not kill him for such an offense, I was banished to live outside Zalanthas until his death. We could make our home in between the boundary of the ancestral wood and his cabin. Mal was much like you. Upfront and honest…Almost to a fault, actually."

"The cabin I came across. It was mixed between human carpentry and elven ecomancy. That's where you lived with him?" Kal asked.

"It was," she smiled.

Is that exile why he gave you permission to stay with me?"

"Yes," she said, "and I haven't been asked to leave the city yet. It'd be the wisest choice actually. My experience with humans is extensive for that very reason."

"And Malex?"

"Dead. His heart gave way two winters ago." Her purple eyes held back the softness of a heart still grieving unhealed by time. "You humans are too mortal sometimes," she whispered, her voice muffled by tears long shed, more morose than sad. She forced a smile. The trees waved with a gentle breeze soothing the tension of the moment.

"I'm sorry. I lost my mother and father some time ago as well. They died traveling up north," Kal put his arm around Sylvara, and their hearts felt heavy in the serenity of the forest.

"C'mon. Let's walk. We'll feel better," she said. The trees whispered their song heavy with the moisture of night.

For a time, they said nothing. The silence soothed them. It took a good hour for the two to encompass the small lake and come to the opposite side of the waterfall before collecting in the lake and continuing on with several streams on the opposite side. In full view, the moon casted small swivels of shifting light.

"Kal, how'd your parents die?"

His eyes narrowed. "My brother said raiders. They robbed the royal caravan up North." Sighing, he paused in contemplation. "And killed them…" his voice trailing off into velvet night.

"And you believe him?" Sylvara asked.

A long pause drew between them in that space between breaths. "No, not anymore." He turned over, putting his arm under his head. He reached out and dimmed the light bauble, but did not extinguish the spell. The silence of his words betrayed the lingering thought of just how well he didn't know his brother. Distrust loomed like the moon herself.

Chapter 7

For several weeks, Tao flew with a small company of men. Tao flew alongside five others. They sat atop blackened skeeters covered in small runes of the same golden material as their armors, hecatium. The skeeter was an insect-inspired clockwork device. Under the seat, a pink magickal fluid glowed. It held the fuel, and the wings of a dragonfly hummed forward, inaudible from the ground. The skeeters were swift, deadly, and in the cover of clouds, indetectable. Above white clouds, they flew. The clouds masked the brightness of the new moon. Every Wizardslayer adorned the same armor except Tao, who sported his arcablade, not the standard lance fastened on the pivoting arm to the right.

The standard lance collected and redirected spell energies, and a gifted Wizardslayer felt when they were the target of magick. No Dim could be a wizardslayer, though no wizardslayer could be mageborne. They existed in a halfway state. They could hear the energies of magick, intuit them, and they could train to redirect ley lines, enchantments, and all manner of spell workings. Their armor could collect these energies at various junctions in the armor: one bracer absorbed, the other released a standard blast of energy. The bracers rotated with several other enchantments combining the mechanistic-technomagick of gears and transmutation to aid in the slaying of an errant wizard and enemy of the Allurian Crown. The gold etching on the black plate provided some basic protection, but a gifted wizard may be able to penetrate it.

Tao felt the pit of his stomach drop. He took an oath to defend the royal family. He grew up with Kal, and was always with him in the forests surrounding the palace grounds. They knew each other as lifelong friends. At the age of eight, Tao joined the Wizardslayers, training from that age until now, a dedicated order answerable only to the crown. Tao had long thought he would serve the Tremayne line, and forever be friends with Kal. In fact, Kalero had even introduced him to his first crush. Now, Tao soared above the clouds ready to kill his friend, a traitor to the Allurian Crown. The hum of the roaring skeeter was virtually silent like the death he sought to bring to his friend, and no moonlight would help Kal this night. They flew, even now, above the Ancestral Wood like a hawk silently knowing where the fish may be plucked from a lake. His unit had been picked by the commander of the Wizardslayers to oversee this mission personally. Closing his eyes, Tao counted each breath, meditating on the night's cool late-summer-wind. The stars shone brightly and his heart grew dark.

Commander Tao held up his hand. Far below, he could feel the node, the magick, the very place of power at the heart of Zalanthas. The five others followed in line. Shutting off the the magickal energy, the skeeter's wings came to a halt and glided in on wind alone. Unbeknownst to elven hubris, the wizardslayers approached in stealth without waking elven patrol below in the tree line. Their arrival in the Ancestral Wood, concealed by the darkness of cloud and tree silhouettes of the forest. Soon, the wind would pick up, and the looming moon exposed them briefly as they exited the cloud cover. They had to move quickly to take advantage of the darkness.

Tao nodded to Zarkas. Zarkas took out a small locket of hair, and placed it on the right side of his gardbrace. A rune on the shoulder absorbed the hair. Taken from Kal's brush in his residence, the small piece of him sent out a faint glowing blue trail. Made worse, the node did not conceal him as it usually did; the bauble intensified the locating spell. Kal's light bauble still hung over his head, a piece of his magick hanging in the world like a beacon, and the use of personal magick intensified Zarkas's locating spell. The blue line sparkled along its edge and periodically flashed. The entire unit closed their visor to night and enchantment. Tao swallowed even harder. Kal was close.

Silently, Tao ordered Zarkas to take point. Following in at the rear, the others led the way. From behind he might not need to see a friend fall by the lances and staves he commanded. Tao rested his thumb on the arcablade unclicking it from the sheath, preparing the blade to be drawn in the coming moments with a heart full of regret.

At the perimeter of the sacred grove and waterfall, the Wizardslayers stopped. They knew as did Kal, the sacredness of this space. They intuitively sensed the underlying magickal energies. In the distance, they saw their prey on the same side. They closed in. Surprise might be the best way to kill a wizard, and in some cases, an arrow would have done them justice, but if a wizard placed wards around his person, the arrow would alarm the victim. As such, the customary

Wizardslayer practice is to open up one's intuition to the presence of magick before moving in on the target. Like a trip wire, the intuition will go off if the wizard senses you. The closer you are, the better off the Wizardslayer, the less time a wizard could work the Art Magick. With the exception of Tao, they did not look to the trees. Tao closed his eyes and bit his lip. They approached closer and closer to their prey making no noise to alert wizard and druidess. Tao held in his breath as the Wizardslayers loomed close. *Could he really do this?*

Some inner feeling snapped in Tao. This was wrong. He was dead wrong. Like a banshee from the Underdark, Tao decided impulsively. "Kal!" Tao screamed as loud as he could.

Then, from the trees, an elven patrol felt the disturbance in the forest. A volley of arrows found their way into two of the gorgets just feet away from the Wizardslayers. The arrows struck the leather guard and opening between neck and breastplate, and two Wizardslayers fell, including Zarkas. The rest of the arrows found the trees as volleys landed in wood without hope of being recovered. A signal arrow whistled through the air, sending alarm to every patrol, and Tao slid down a tree occasionally looking around the trunk. "Kal! Watch out!" he screamed once again.

Sylvara rose instantly, knife in hand. In that moment, she thought herself dead, but Kal's magickal instincts kicked into high gear as did Zarkas's gift at the end of his life. He held his wound in his throat with one arm, and held a crystal globe in one hand that he smashed on the ground. A shield spell encircled them. The arrows bounced off the blue forcefield. Protecting the others, the arrows recoiled off it, the wood buckling back into straight and still sticks that gently fell at the shield's base.

From his hands, Kal shot frozen ice at the approaching Wizardslayer, but aimed it at the ground. The Wizardslayer pointed the lance-now-morphed-into-halberd. Sylvara saw the magick being redirected as the Wizardslayer tried to move forward. He leveraged his halberd up, pushing the spell up and away. Sylvara flipped the dagger into her hand, ready to throw. The Wizardslayer slipped on the icy ground. As he fell back, Sylvara threw the dagger into the visor. But as one fell, two more immediately pounced, but now Kal fell back trying to regain his balance.

Calling upon the spirit of the weapon, Kal levitated the handle staff of the halberd and animated it, investing his will to survive in an object more skilled at combat than himself. The true name of skill and his own power came to him, almost like a gate flapping in howling wind. The magick came uncertain and in bolts of intense feeling. Like the lashing of a whip, the skill came into the hovering halberd and then receded. Under its own power, the weapon danced parrying the attack of two of them giving him enough time to rise to his feet. Not skilled in combat, Kal backed away from the Wizardslayer buying more time. He bought them a few seconds, if that. The Wizardslayers before him easily parried the attacks, and the spell of weapon animation seemed more of a nuisance than a threat.

Reluctance in his heart, Tao unfastened his breast plate. "I'm coming Kal" He dashed for his unit. In that very moment, Tao finally felt right as if balance in his heart restored itself. In his vision's field, he highlighted members of his unit in the combat vision. His mind found renewed focus in the memory of friendship. A life of regret suddenly purged in the tranced-state of combat's purity.

The two Wizardslayers approached two by two next to each other. From behind, they heard the clang of steel, and Tao's blade clanged with their brother-in-arms behind, yet they now stood divided against a formidable foe from the rear and Kalero Tremayne, the hero of the Eastern Gate in front of them. As they backed away, Sylvara found a branch. She called out to the forest, and her skin became hard as ironwood, the branch smoothed into a staff. Her hair blew wildly like the fauna and ferns around her in storm wind. Her magick felt as steady and firm as the roots that drove down deep.

"Listen," she warned Kal before speeding off for one of the opponents on one side. She bought Kal not more time, but only one opponent. Ironwood and steel clashed behind him, leaving the Wizardslayer slowly stalking Kal back into the wood. What had she meant by listen?

"I am your Lord. Stop this at once!" Kal commanded.

The Wizardslayer scoffed. "I don't bargain with usurpers," he said mockingly, "Besides, you're second-born. Killing you ensures the peace."

Oak after oak, Kal put tree after tree in front of them. "I could dance like this all day, little prince," the wizardslayer said. The Wizardslayer cut the enchanted branches dispelling the magic entanglement of vines and wood as Kal backed up.

Kal did not talk but opened his senses. Tao and Sylvara still fought, yet he was far from them. This Wizardslayer wanted the prince's head for himself.

Tao swung upward, arching the curved singing blade into the halberd. He danced with his comrade, Gumatra.

"Why brother?" Gumatra asked. As he crossed blades with Tao, Gumatra eyes grew inquisitive, sad, and irritated.

Tao had only replied "the Oath." Tao had taken the oath as Commander of the Wizardslayers to protect the Tremayne line. Now, they stood violating it. A family divided cannot stand. Still, Gumatra was skilled with his halberd and kept the master swordsman at bay with large swinging arcs.

Finally, the blade had cut through the shaft splicing metal and wooden frame sewn together by powerful magick. As the shaft broke, a slight blue sizzle of lightning faded, and Gumatra fell to his knees. In front of them, the sounds of battle could be heard.

"Yield," Tao ordered, "Stop this foolish mission. Hiraeus would never approve."

"And yet, I serve his kin." Gumatra bowed his head. "Kill me. It'll be an honorable end. Either I fall by your blade to ensure one Tremayne, or I kill a prince to serve another," Gumatra said. Tao did not hesitate. Through the armor, his arcablade hummed with the vibrancy of moonlight, and Tao killed his comrade.

Sylvara's ancient magick made her one with the forest. Her attacker, while skilled, could not predict when she would flip, jump, and dodge the large attacks nor how the forest would transform brush and growth into solid ground. In the forest, the Wizardslayer had no advantage. He had forced her into the clearing by the banks of the lake. He could maneuver his halberd, and deflect her attacks, but he lost some of his footing in the murky mud. From the trees above, arrows flew only to hit the large force field surrounding them. The patrol could not get close. One of the elven guards even jumped on it figuring that the enchantment might only be for their arrows. He was wrong, and flipped off standing ready should signs of the field's collapse prove imminent.

As the halberd blade drew near, it would nullify some of Sylvara's transformed skin. In the intensity of the melee, the Wizardslayer drew back the halberd and a small draw sliced into Sylvara's shoulder. She winced in pain, and batted the halberd's shaft away. Striking down, she clonked the helm as hard as she could. The enchanted wood broke, but not without effect. The piece that flew off the helm transformed back into the former branch. The Wizardslayer grabbed his head, instinctively dropping the halberd in the process. Blood poured into his eyes, half blinded he tried to get some distance, the head wound ringing in his ears. Morphing out from the gauntlet, a mini-crossbow formed with golden darts already loaded into its enchanted chamber. Frantically, the Wizardslayer fired them, and they came at Sylvara with mechanized speed. She dove for cover into the lake. The darts hit close, whizzing past her head and striking a partially submerged tree root. In the panic, however, she dropped her own power she called upon.

Durkin, the last remaining Wizardslayer, was far from the battle. The tree canopy concealed the full moonlight, and the Wizardslayer knew the prince had only trained with ceremonious rapiers at court. Rounding a tree, Durkin found Kalero standing ready. Kal spoke the name of lightning, and felt the magick churn like a furnace of the Allurian destroyer. For an instant, the power hung in his hands swirling and maddening. Kal launched a lightning strike and hurled wind at Durkin simultaneously. Extending the halberd, Durkin caught the magickal energies on the tip of his weapon, and deflected the bolt into the air while pushed back by the gale of wind. Kalero hoped that would work. On route, the elven patrol saw the bolt of lightning stream into the sky above. Then, the arrows came. Kalero's gamble had paid off. The elven retinue guarding them had found at least one intruder way outside the shield. Would they come in time?

Lifting his arm, Durkin activated the morphing shield on the gauntlet, and activated the mini crossbow. Kalero had more time, now. He reached out to the forest listening to the ebb and flow of magick. In his mind, he received an intuition, a blessing-as-voice. *Listen.* The web of life was around him, and he found the plant energies willing to change for him, the treesong commanded him to weave and bop in the storm of conflict. His spindling fingers wove the lifeforce around him, collecting it as one did the aroma of newly baked bread. In his mind, he spoke the language of making and change, urging the new form of life of the ferns and grass around him to change into ironwood thorns. Woven into a protection spell, the thorny vines reached out even to Sylvara and then to Tao. The magick came sudden, out of nowhere, and unlike his earlier spells, this had no control behind it. The spell encased them all. His magick knew friend from foe, and even some of the retinue charging Durkin had paths of ironwood thorns changing before them as they ran.

Durkin shot back his volley of tiny arrows. As one of the guards charged him, the arrows found their mark and the approaching elven guards fell. Others came from the trees. By now, a horn had sounded, and Durkin knew he had only seconds. He could still see Kalero, an emanating glow reaching beyond through the thicket of sorcery. Spinning the anti-magickal halberd in his position, the blade easily reverted ironwood thorns into grass and fern. However, when he drew his attention away from protecting his head, several more arrows found their mark, one in his side, the other finding his shoulder. Durkin winced in pain, but this pain only accelerated his attack. Sprinting towards Kal, the Wizardslayer flipped and jumped over and through the enchanted growth of ironwood thorns. When he came into the small circle of Kalero's casting, vines ran from Kalero's arms up into a tree. The arms became vines. Kal's vines stretched to the tops of one of the nearby dead trees, and he yanked hard as soon as Durkin came in view. A large trunk of tree barreled straight for him. In that instant, Kal had timed it well. One second sooner, Kalero would be dead; one second later, he would have missed.

The trunk struck dead on target. Crushed, Durkin screamed, and his body jerked in death. Kal darted back towards the commotion. The battle could still be heard. Rushing to his feet, Kal sprinted with staff in hand. Beside him, Sylvara's bodyguards sprinted and flipped through the trees.

More arrows formed in the gauntlet. She saw the second volley enter the air. Suddenly, vines surrounded her, and she could hear the arrows dink off of the ironwood. In the protected cocoon of willed magick, she sensed forest, life, and energy coming together in a will not of her own making. The magick felt solid and reassuring as if Kal had listened to the Ancestral Wood. Some thing or someone had tapped into the forest and its energy, but that energy was a gift, not taking and ripped apart from without. In her heart, she knew. She didn't even need to speak his name. Kalero had started to listen to the very creation around him as she instructed. Finally, the Magelord understood, or at the very least understood the elven relationship to nature.

Flight of the Ravenhawk

Taking off his helm, the Wizardslayer pointed his weapon at the cocoon of ironwood thorns. The enchanted magick faded, and he morphed the halberd into a spear as he pointed it at Sylvara. Just then, Tao flipped down. With sword in hand, he deflected the spear blow against the enchanted arcablade. Blue lightning sparked and fizzled. In this sheer moment of sacrifice, the guards and Kal saw Tao's act. Tao had distracted the guard from Sylvara just long enough. Wasting no time, grass vines and bark snatched Sylvara on the ground as iced formed and chilled beneath her skin hastening her retreat to safety gliding straight into Kalero's arms. She stood swallowing pride and honor.

"Stop this foolishness, Kai," Tao screamed, taking off his helm. "We took an oath to protect the Tremayne line." He hoped his words might find their way home to Kai's dedicated heart, and held his sword downward.

Kai's blood-stained gash seemed better, but speckles of red and black dotted his darkened face. "I was not a favorite at Court like you. I serve the Tremayne King, not the line." Kai spun his weapon with martial prowess, and attempted to strike Tao's head. In that moment, Tao spun exerting his breath, his heart heavy.

"And what if the brother would make the better King?" Tao asked his brother-in-arms.

For a moment, the combat paused. Each warrior relaxing with exhausted breath. The elven patrol now landing behind Kal and Sylvara. "Even then, it does not matter." Kai looked on Tao with regret. "Kalero is not the Mageking."

Tao circled his arms, grabbed the hilt, and readied himself. "You were a good friend Kai."

"Aye," Kai responded.

To no avail, Tao deflected the blow as Kai's fidelity deflected what seemed treasonous. Kai and Tao danced as expert warriors, and the elven guards looked on with fascinated caution. They had never seen the human Wizardslayers up close, and they were stunned at the martial prowess these two warriors displayed with the morphing polearm and arcablade. When one of the guards looked to Sylvara's eyes to raise his bow, she simply shook her head, and quietly Kal nodded. They were not to interfere.

Kai fought Tao to the shore, but while Tao could not get into reach and land a blow, his sword took flight to meet the spear blade with incredible ease. More sparks flew like the cinders from a great blue flame. A fury of blows came as

Kai instantly launched another attack once Tao parried. Tao had to get inside. Sidestepping a lunge, Tao spun and struck the throat. Immediately, he dropped his sword to catch Kai as he fell. Yet, in one instant of compassion, Kai betrayed his friendship to duty. From his gauntlet, he launched a spell beacon.

"No," Tao screamed in unison with Kal, but it was too late. An intense white orb shot forward from his Kai's hand and then his body stilled.

As Kai's eyes grew white and lifeless, Tao saw his mouth utter words. "A good death," Kai whispered. He smiled. Tao held him in his arms.

Both Kal and Tao looked pale. Looking up, the white light rippled out on the night sky as if the energy sought its master. The ripples roared like thunder, they roared straight into the heart of Venda. The guards and Sylvara looked at both of them not understanding their alarm.

"Kal...Kal?" Sylvara had to shake him. "Kal, what is that?" She pointed skyward.

"The spell beacon records the mission details of the unit, Kai's memories, and sends back these images and thoughts to command." Sighing, Kal continued. "Here, the spell beacon is meant only for the King. My brother will know where to find me now, but that's the secondary function of a spell beacon. It's launched when the mission fails, and signals another intention."

"What's the primary function of that spell, Kal?" Sylvara asked. She was losing patience, and her body tensed with fear.

With measured calm, Tao looked straight into her eyes. "The primary function of a spell beacon is to call in bombardment from the skyfleet should a ground unit fail." Turning his head to Kal, Tao said, "I didn't know Kal, I swear. I only knew they wanted you dead. I did not know that Zalanthas was its intended back up plan."

"They probably dispatched the skyfleet once they learned where I was. We have to learn how much time we have until they arrive."

****

From the tower's edge, Darnashi stood glancing out over the full-mooned sky. Next to him stood the Prime Magus. Both could feel the spell beacon. The memories of that conflict flooded their minds.

"Resourceful, my brother."

Darnashi, now healed, concealed part of his exposed skeleton from onlookers. His hood concealed the bits of darkened flesh metal, and glints of polished silver and steel scattered across his body. In Court, he made little effort to hide his brother's wounds. The treachery of his face reminded him of his failure to deal adequately with his brother. His one eye glowed intensely seeing into the astral world overlaying this one. The magick so far away stood out like phosphorus burning with the intensity of ten thousand suns. "They failed because Tao betrayed us." He replayed those images. He swatted away a firefly that landed on his shoulder. "Level the city. I already dispatched the fleet. And mark Tao for death, twenty thousand gold crowns on his head." Folding both hands, Darnashi retreated into the keep, but the Prime Magus's words caught him in the door.

"Sire, won't that leave Venda vulnerable to attack?" the Prime Magus asked.

"From whom?" King Darnashi asked. A smile of lust and power parted his lips. For a long time, the elven Kingdom had been a nuisance, and tensions were high enough between them. What better excuse for war than concealing his brother? By the time the skyfleet arrived, Kal would be long gone, and Kal would learn that no matter where he went, the price of his life would be the death of others—the very others he picked over his own family's ambition. He put faith, the very faith of their mother before the station of his birth and Alluria itself. Kal had picked to serve Creation and the Source before family. His mother had always loved Kal more, and now they could be united in death, counting the fallen souls to the Pure Light itself cast down by Darnashi's power.

"Since my brother loves the Lightdweller faith so much he would forget his own station and family, let's start eradicating Lightdweller Temples. Purge them in Alluria, and we'll be sure to destroy them to the south as we pass overhead to victory."

"Aye, ma'lord," the Prime Magus bowed as Darnashi retreated back into the keep.

The Prime Magus descended into his chambers far beneath. For a time, he did not speak when he arrived. Witness sat perched on one of the banisters in a way that a human body should not be perched. His face was made beautiful by the sacrificed woman, but his mannerism resembled a predatory bird.

"I'm sending you on your mission, now. The Wizardslayers failed."

"Of course, Master." His words hissed out of her mouth like a serpent. "May I use my powers in pursuit of your vision?"

The Prime Magus eyed him with suspicion. To give a demon permission like that was unwise, but he still asked in respect nonetheless. "Yes, yes, but do not reveal your true nature, even to Kal."

"He'll know. That, I have no question of, Master."

"Is he considered that powerful by the Underdark?"

The demon shook his head. "Not yet. Power is not measured by spellcasting. It's measured in deeds."

The Prime Magus slumped in his seat, his black robes rubbing against the blood red satin of his study, and his hand nervously rubbing his chin. In the distance, a clock ticked, ticking away as if gnawing at him. He could not get the spell beacon images out of his head: betrayal, friendship, and the manner in which Kal could spellcast. He had not gestured, nor spoken words of true making and change. He'd only pointed those fingers, and they became wood, vine, and plant life. Had he become a mage of pure thought? Kal's magick seemed too effortless, like drawing breath to a newborn. Something had changed, and if left unchecked, then Kal could ruin his plans.

"The King has ordered the destruction of all Lightdweller Temples." Witness smiled directly at him. "No doubt there will be refugees.

If I know Kal, he'll make his way to wherever they flee, one way or the other. Hide amongst them. I'll inform his majesty that one of my agents will travel with them, and that may be the best way to find him. We'll put the rabble at his feet, no matter where he goes." The Prime Magus put his hand on his cheek. He was exhausted.

"It will be done. I'll take my leave of you and acquire what I need from your servants," Witness said.

Witness climbed the stairs and stopped one of the servants requesting a formal dress, a small hand purse, the small fortune of 11,000 crowns, and for the upper chambers to draw a hot bath. A noble lady, dim from the minor houses of the Allurian Empire, will flee with the refugees of the persecution, come to their aid, and like the Prime Magus said, kill Kalero Tremayne. What his master had not said was *when*, and it was this free time, the time sent to kill a wizard that Witness would serve his *other master*, the one of the nameless dark, a being so old it had no name in the language of making and change. That Master wanted Kalero Tremayne dead, too. Of course, it also wanted the mortal King Darnashi to rule Alluria for the time being, but for reasons that no mortal or demon could understand. The Underdark moved in its own way, steady and purposeful as Light moved in the still silence. Witness knew the will of his true master, and dared not question what he did not understand. That was not his purpose. It was also why he had been the one that the summoning spell had called up from the Great Wheel to which all demons spawn and return in the endless cycle of reincarnation. The nameless dark had spoken *for the time being. And for the time being*, Witness would serve the Prime Magus.

The Prime Magus coordinated with the King. The hapless damsel and dim noblewoman Irina Corovan, a confessed Lightdweller fled two days earlier as the Vendan Guard corralled the believers, burned their hidden temple in a neighborhood North of the Damask one. Like its counterpart, the Temple of Shariaton had been underground, underneath a winery, and they had taken refuge in the connecting cellars. King Darnashi's scryers foretold the point of their retreat, and so, among them, Irina Corovan cowered in fear. She saw King Darnashi, personally, take several heads with an animated sword of magickal energy and laughed as the believers fled. The Vendan Guards chased them, and fellow citizens watched in horror as some of them were hung from the gas-powered lights in the city streets. Dangling like festival decorations, the bodies signaled the end of any toleration the Lightdwellers shared within the empire. The survivors saw their homes burned. On the walls, guards launched arrows into the fleeing horde. The guards behind chased them, sometimes trampling the elderly and young alike. For some time, the Lightdwellers had been tolerated, somewhat, but not always. They still lived in fear of the occasional pogrom. Now, the King had all but signed their death warrant in the city walls. Soon, the guards would find Lightdweller paraphernalia on those the state deemed dangerous. Darnashi would clean his city, ensure loyalty if by nothing else than fear alone, and remove all threats and sympathizers loyal to his brother. There would never be another Tao.

Irina Corovan watched witnessing the horror, the bloodshed, and knew that only thirty percent were intended to live from the King's command. Several roadways had been cleared to make it easier to herd the rushing flood of refugees. When they reached the city walls, the King halted the advance of his forces. Adorning the same armor as before, he changed into the dragon, chasing the Lightdwellers out of the Eastern Gate. His form, now hideous and plated with the same silvery metal that covered his wounds openly, shadowed over the group of twenty or so that remained. "If you see my brother, tell him that death awaits his people. I'll eventually come for you all, so you'd better make haste," Darnashi hissed. His voice boomed and echoed over them. Above him, ten large airships of the skyfleet casted an even larger shadow, and tiny skeeters of patrolling Wizardslayers held their lances at the ready, buzzing about the large white ships like flies around pestilence. Huge furnaces of magicktech bellowed and fueled the bulbous monstrosities. Darnashi had mobilized death to follow him. The Allurians were going to war.

Chapter 8

"Honestly, Kal, I didn't know," Tao urged a second time.

"I believe you." Kal picked up the arcablade and handed it to Tao. "Thank you for your friendship." Taking the sword, Tao half-smiled. "And loyalty."

Tao bowed in silence, and took his place behind the Prince. Tao surrendered his hands, but Sylvara's guards made no move.

Speaking in elven, Sylvara commanded her retinue to find the king. More guards would be coming now, and it was urgent they speak. Kal placed his hand on Sylvara's shoulder. She took it and held it. Kalero sighed heavily, and did not speak. Looking up, he could see the spell beacon radiating outward, its circle growing larger in the distance. He had to find out. At best, it would only communicate the memories of the mission collective if they were linked or individually. At worst, it would call in the skyfleet.

Sylvara mouthed, "Go." Then, as if by reflex, Kalero became the ravenhawk. In his mind, he spoke the true naming and found the form still etched in both memory and in his very essence. For once changed, the changed form stays with the name so changed. Unlike the gifted power of the Ancestral Wood, this power was determined, willful, and defiant. The magick came from without to alter what was within. Outstretched arms became obsidian wings. The darks wings became like folds of dark fabric. The magick echoed and reverberated on the skin. An echoing "caw" permeated the sacred grove. Parting clouds, the ravenhawk saw the expanse of moonlight giving way to the blanket of clouds obscuring its light and warmth. Wind and thermal pockets shot up from the ground, lifting and pushing Kal. Effortlessly, the ravenhawk could feel the tremble of wind, and for a short time, Kal forgot his troubles. In his thoughts, he called forth the might of the spellwind, and like a weather-worker aboard a barge, he sent forward the wind to guide flight, empowering the bird's speed to enchanted speeds. For several hours, he hurled himself magickally into the night half suspecting another patrol, another squad of elite troops to find him and him alone. Like any hawk, the ravenhawk had tremendous eyesight. Even more, the eyes could penetrate the darkness and even gave light to where none was, a secret known to mages who wish to see in the darkness and take this form.

In the eyes of the ravenhawk, however, Kal found what he did not want to find. On the edge of the horizon and above the forest canopy of these ancient woods, the Allurian Skyfleet. Ten ships, five destroyers, and support vessels flew slowly toward Zalanthas. With a heavy heart, the ravenhawk spun around. Picking his bearing, the ravenhawk entered the mist of clouds, and once again, called the spellwind at his back and made haste to Zalanthas.

That night, when he arrived, he landed on the windowsill of the Librarian. The small man pushed his spectacles up the bridge of his nose, and hobbled over to him when Kal became man once more. Both hands covered Kal's face, and slowly he slid down the wall. Tears filled his eyes. It took an hour for him to find his voice again. With haste, he wrote: *The fleet comes, Master Librarian*." The Librarian brought over a map, and Kal knew instantly in his memory where they had been, and what course they had set. A ravenhawk knows when other birds compete for the same hunting grounds, and now the predators anger held fast the determination of his throat.

"As I suspected. Every elf worth his salt in these woods could feel that disturbing magick," the Librarian retorted as if insulted by the very air in which the vessels flew. The Librarian called one of the archivists and sent a note to the King immediately. The young elf nodded knowing fully well the message contained, but sealed with the Librarian's own seal, a book bound open under a shining sun.

"How many must die because of me?"

The Librarian hit Kalero hard with his cane. "Oww," Kal said, instinctively.

"Now listen here. These Vendans will need a King, a man of heart and conscience. That's you Kalero Tremayne. The time of the sobbing scholar who feels the weight of the world and the pulling of his heart is over. Cast aside the turmoil you feel. It's time to lead."

Kal's hands shook, but steadied at the old elf's words. Wiping his tears, he collected himself. The anger of the predatory bird left him, his humanity making him vulnerable.

"By the Source, your timing couldn't be more perfect." The Librarian poured Kal some tea, and sat across from him. "In moments, the War Council will meet, and we'll be escorted over to the King. Until then, feel all you need over a cup of tea because after this, Kal, there's no feeling this weight without the whole human quarter and elven kingdom watching." Sighing, Kal inhaled deeply and exhaled his hesitation. In order to protect the Alluria he loved, others must die. It was easier said than done.

****

Vanaxx Quintoriel called everyone into his throne room regardless of the late hour. Commotion sounded outside. As the guards were raised and patrols heightened, the Council of Lords was summoned. Lord Vetranalaa stood slender and fair, his skin nearly white as snow with green piercing eyes. To his left, Lord Shurdanatos crossed his arms. His skin was as black as the robes he bore, but his silver hair was as white as his colleague's. Lady Anarkana flowed into the room with unearthly grace and poise, the second oldest to King Vanaxx himself. Her hair shone like reflective oak by the light of bauble and torches. Behind them, Princess Sylvara, the newly-elected Abbot Whittaker, known to everyone alongside Dorn, and lastly Ellex – the archivist – followed the Librarian. The refugees elected Dorn, now, as their voice in the elven city.

"I've called you all because the guards have brought it to my attention that Allurian forces have attacked us in the Ancestral Wood. At the heart of our own node, even. I ask that all of us speak Basic so as to include all parties here."

Lord Vetranalaa and Shurdanatos exchanged glances with each other and Lady Anarkana. The Elven Lords looked nervous. Tensions rose.

"Why?" Vetranalaa asked. "Why would they attack us here?"

"We know why." King Vanaxx motioned for the glamour of Ellex Sablon to walk forward. Anarkana's eyes narrowed, discerning powerful complexity and workings of magick. "This is the Archivist Ellex Sablon, who some may know, some may not." He paused looking at the council elders. "I gave this man specific permission to remain hidden amongst his people. If you could…"

As if plucking away an unclasped cloak from his neck, Prince Kalero turned the glamour about his person off. The magick left him in an instant and felt like a soldier's sweat meeting the air for the first time once the armor is cast off. Small speckles of fairy-like dust evaporated into the air as if made of vanishing fireflies. He stood in his white mage robes, black vest, and carried his white and red staff. "I am Prince Kalero Tremayne, second-born to the throne of Alluria, and Magelord."

"My spies in Venda claim that your brother has been tearing up the world in search of you," Anarkana said. She turned to King Vanaxx. "You hid him?"

"I came here out of design. I had no purpose in coming here, yet this is where I found myself, and for the past few weeks I have been here with permission, searching out ways to defeat my brother."

Vetranalaa turned to Shurdanatos. Shurdanatos uncrossed his arms. "Great, we've been harboring an usurper."

"Careful with your words, elven lord," Dorn warned. "That's my Prince and next King of Alluria who would more than likely bring a peace even you could benefit from." Brother Whittaker nudged him in the arm to keep from escalating the tension in the room. Once angered, elves rarely calmed so quickly as their human counterparts.

Vetranalaa and Shurdanatos seemed to ignore the human representative. Vetranalaa swatted at Shurdanatos and his words. "You know very well that Alluria has long wanted control of the Ancestral Wood. The mageborne want access to our knowledge, and the sacred space of power, the power of lands to fuel their war machine. It was only a matter of time."

"Perhaps." Anarkana turned to Prince Kalero. "And what attacked us?"

Sighing, Prince Kalero knew the answer would not be popular. "Wizardslayers," he said. Glances were exchanged; they all knew that the only reason Wizardslayers would be sent here would be to kill *him*. "The last one shot a spell beacon into the air. They were sent to kill me, and now my brother will launch a full-on-assault on Zalanthas now."

"How do you figure?" Dorn asked.

"A spell beacon is used to call in bombardment from the skyfleet should a small precision strike fail," Anarkana turned to Ventranalaa and returning the answer to Dorn's question with the force of necessity and ridicule rolled into one. "I have returned from ravenhawk form. I saw the fleet myself."

Itching his brow, Vetranalaa ran the numbers in his head. "Three days, maybe four if they are coming."

"I'd say your estimates are right," Kal said.

Turning uncomfortably to her father, Sylvara crossed her arms. "Father, should we not get Kal out of here? They may be only after him," Sylvara said.

"If it were only that simple," Anarkana said. "My spy network knows that Lightdwellers were chased out of the city by the dragon-form of King Darnashi and the city guard. Only about twenty or so made it out of the Eastern Gate. They slaughtered some of the rest as they fled. The Kingdom is declaring an open war on the Lightdwellers and us. The refugees were instructed to find you and tell you that your brother is coming for you." Her words bit into Kal's soul.

"Zalanthas would've been included regardless of whether I allowed the Prince Kalero to remain or not. For years, I've opened our lands to the Lightdweller faith to find safety. There's always been a human quarter in Zalanthas since Alluria's creation." King Vanaxx raised his voice to emphasize this last point in an attempt to unite the politicking elven lords.

"The monster!" Brother Whittaker muttered under his breath.

Closing his eyes, Kal placed his hands on the oaken table and bent down. "What do you want to do?" Kal asked Vanaxx softly.

"I've already ordered the evacuation. The Librarian's power can guide the people safely out of the city into the Underrealm. Is that okay with you old friend?" Vanaxx turned to the Librarian.

Without saying a word, the Librarian nodded in agreement. The Librarian's eyes met the King without flinching. A look passed between them, almost as if they had knew each other as equals for centuries. "I'll see to the raising of the wall and towers, too."

"Thank you," King Vanaxx said, and the Librarian departed with haste.

Vanaxx pointed to Ventranalaa. "Ready the Griffin Riders." Then he pointed to Shurdanatos, "Ready all the mageborne we have, especially anyone with weather-working and warding. They'll man the towers."

Anarkana interrupted. "Griffin riders will not be much work against the Allurian Skyfleet. We should run; evacuate the city in its entirety."

"If I may..." Kal walked forward. "We have Skeeters. Commander Tao and I could dress in the Wizardslayer armor, board some of the ships, and cause a little damage. Buy you some time."

"The hunted would become the hunter," Shurdanatos muttered in disbelief.

From the shadows, Tao appeared. Shocked, the elven lords cursed differently each in Elven at the interruption. Looking over his shoulder to meet Tao's gaze, Kal smirked at the presence of his friend, protecting and watching from the shadows unbeknownst to even the elven guards. That made the threat ever more serious. "You'd be killed in Wizardslayer armor. It would drain you of any strength you could muster," Tao said. "I didn't betray my order to see you killed needlessly."

"You betrayed no one," Kal said. He placed his arm on Tao's shoulder. "I'd not be killed this close to a node. I could sustain myself long enough."

Anarkana shook her head. "No, your ability to defend your *Schata*." She paused. "I cannot think of the word....Ah. Your title. That must come on a different day human prince." Shurdanatos nodded in agreement. They talked and dismissed Kal as quickly as he had revealed himself. He could clearly see that now because the elven word to refer to a King's domain was *Onera*. *Schata* referred to the property of a lowborn.

Immediately, Kal went into perfect elven. "Enough!" Stamping his staff down, a brilliant light encompassed the room, his rage fueling the brilliant flash. Kal's hair moved of its own accord as the rage resonated in his words.

"Schakeera vanesti pra'kwa leznetoba na'la sobretan ye *Onera*, na'la sobretan ye scrongok Reva'taldenday." He repeated his words exactly in basic. "This is not about titles, nor about my claim to Alluria's throne." He paused again making sure to emphasize to the newly red-faced lords that the human prince spoke elven perfectly, flawlessly. He bent reverently putting his head to staff and closed his eyes. "It's about the safety of Zalanthas. And, I'm not to be addressed as human prince. I am *Prince Kalero*," he said in a balanced silence that was unnerving.

Kal paused looking both to Dorn and Brother Whittaker, "Bring the humans into the square. I'll address them myself. I'll call on all those able-bodied to assist the elves in defense of our new home. Let me make that request of them myself." The highborn elves exchanged curious glances at the mention of our new home.

Sylvara turned to her father, and spoke the soft and subtle tongue of elvish and whispered. "Father, I can be much more useful. Send me to the Dwarven Mountains to the East. Certainly, they've got ships similar to the Allurians. They're obligated under treaties signed long ago to come to our aid."

"Nobody is faster than you on a Griffin," Vanaxx returned. "It's a good idea. Go.

Be swift. I'd thought to call on King Thayumeer the Bold."

Immediately, she rose with purpose. Vanaxx took her arm and spoke softly to her. "I regret your exile, daughter. If we're to do battle, forgive an old man and his old ways. I'd not have the anger between us, nor any arrangement that separates us now, especially with whatever fate may befall us. You do your station proud, and you'll make a fine queen someday."

She smiled, "Someday?" Her words changed back to common.

Shifting to Kal, Vanaxx looked approvingly, but he had words on the tip of his tongue. "You intend to stay?"

"I've been running long enough from Nash. Besides, if I can do anything, it'd be to slow down the Skyfleet. Give people more time to evacuate." Brother Whittaker left the room to gather people in the Human Quarter for prayer.

"Then, address your people, Prince." Vanaxx sat up from his throne. "We'll plan our defenses. Do what you can to help."

"We'll send able-bodied men to help. May the Goddess Queen watch over us," Kal said. He faced the elven lords, and in elven he said, "All of us." He let those words sink into their minds. As he left, the lords bowed their heads, but their eyes pierced him with cold, steely eyes.

"Indeed, may the Source be with us all." King Vanaxx pulled out the Star of Galadrana revealing his Lightdweller faith—the same pendant Kal wore. The elven lords noticed the king came down from the throne to shake Kal's hand. Like a best-friend, Kal knew what King Vanaxx was doing. By defying protocol, Vanaxx reassured the elven lords of the confidence and station Kal occupied in his mind. Kal clasped his arm in honor and affection as an *equal*.

Chapter 9

Outside, the walk was long. With the glamour lifted, Kal carried tension in his chest. For the record, he hated politics, preferring the ivory tower of his Academy of Magery, the almond-like smell of parchment covers and leather-bound tomes of ancient lore. In his heart, though heavy, he knew his place could not be the library archives any longer. Slowly, he walked in tempo with his staff hitting the street. Each tap brought forward flashes of golden light. The chaos of the world ensued by his bloodthirsty necromantic brother. He found the square of the human quarter. Brother Whittaker had just finished leading the group in a quick prayer. Before him, he found the steps of the Library where the square ended and the elven sections of the city started. He no longer wore the common threads of the archivist, Ellex Sablon. Several gasped. Many knew him. Instead, he wore his white robes and staff of his station.

"Today, I come to you as someone who has always been by your side. Some may have known me and my work in the Archives as Ellex

Sablon, a glamour, an illusion to prevent my likeness from being found. I came here by the Source's will, and for the past few weeks kept hidden by the powers of this place and the gentle will of King Vanaxx of House Quintoriel." Slow murmurs of astonishment gave pause to the care in which Kalero chose his words.

"Now, I come to you as your prince to ask two things of you." With arms stretched wide, Kalero beckoned them. "Elven forces will defend this city, their home. I ask that all males of age take up sword against the Allurian Skyfleet headed this way. Alluria threatens us once again, but this time, we defend our home." Kalero now raised his voice, assisted in the part by an echoing effect imbuing his voice. "We'll not abandon the kindness of the elves, nor the sanctity of our faith. We will not go silently into the night; we will not recede into the darkness of our own despair and persecution. Now, at this moment, take an oath with me that tonight and for the rest of our lives we stand with our elven brethren." The crowd erupted into rancorous approval. "I pledge this to you all. My power is not for me, but for the safety of all, I stand with you!" Again, eruptions of approval screamed so much that the elven Highborn could hear them throughout the entire city.

At the sounds of the crowds, Kalero raised up the staff, pointed it at the clear night sky giving way to the new day's light, and lightning struck it. In the cloudless patch from above, the lightning came; magickal power surged through by his will alone. He need not speak the words that called forth change and making. Instead, he willed it for all to see.

Taking hold of the staff, Kalero closed his eyes. His words were inaudible. His whispers were soft, and his head bowed. Prayer, Kalero believed, was a special type of power all its own on behalf of that which gives being to all. Private devotion need not be public, but one must take the time to reorient oneself towards balance, towards peace. One must fill the void and gap between one's ego-filled-mind and world with the peace, with the Light for which the religion's namesake demanded of its believers. Without that self-sacrificing love at the heart of its teaching being lived by its practitioners, the Lightdweller faith meant little if anything. Even the calmest ocean must weather hardened rocks. Like the sea, Kalero the Magelord, now commanded others to do battle, to weather the sharp-edged forces of evil. Sometimes, peace demanded just action and limited violence.

Flight of the Ravenhawk

"Next, and perhaps the most difficult, I ask you not to run, but to fight and assist in the evacuation of these lands. Take what little you need, and make your way to the archives. Once there, the Librarian will organize the evacuation and volunteers. He'll know how best to instruct you all about what needs to be done."

With the speech concluded, he joined the people in the square at street level. People wanted to touch his white robes, and he let them. Despite not liking politicking, Kalero realized his presence was needed here—a measure of reassurance that not everyone would abandon the Dim to ruin. More than ever before, the world needed change, and Kalero finally understood that to think about the world and the change it required are two different things. To enact those ideas is quite another task, a task he had avoided for far too long. With his talents, he should've been more capable of discerning how pragmatic he should've been with his mind's attentions turned toward the abstractions of peace and understanding. The reform Alluria needed required leadership that only he could provide.

****

The Librarian descended a dank staircase into a dark chamber in the library. Moisture thickened this far down into the chambers underneath the city, and the smell of almond-crusted pages had long gone. In these chambers, several levers linked to chain locks rusted on a wooden wall. Tapping his cane, the Librarian released enchanted locks. Created long ago, these magicks were time-locked, and entrusted to the Master Librarian. Secret doors lowered the bookcases of the library into chambers far beneath. Steel cases clanked. Ancient books were sealed in vaults designed for this very purpose, enchanted by powerful magick; the lore would continue on even in a world where no elf remained alive, but only the worthy could raise them again. Opposite him, several guards worked the release of giant boulders connected to chains on giant wheels and pulleys. Each system of weights raised a tower and between each tower a connecting wall.

Atop the city, large towers of stone emerged from the forest floor, and on top of these towers a large crystal jutted out fixed to a seat with two control arms, similar to the lightning cannons on Allurian destroyers. These locks and pulleys released magickal spells of transformation for the city's defenses. Glowing branches came together as boulders and ironwood vines surrounded them, and the sacred Underrealm roots raised the walls of the city as high as the ancient red woods, oaks, and arboreal plants. The lowborn and the humans moved supplies underneath the Archives. Under Zalanthas, a network of caverns and magick formed for miles. In a long chain of hands, humans and elves passed food, water, seeds, and crops down the line and into the Underrealm. Humans learned the secret to which the human quarter had never known; the real power of the elven kingdom came not from the ancestral wood alone, but also the powers of earth and water that carved the Underrealm far below they witnessed as they entered this underrealm underneath the library.

In the sacred grove for the past two days Kalero sat on a rock before the waterfalls. Nobody disturbed him. In his wizard's eye, Kalero opened himself up to the listening first taught to him by Sylvara's primordial Druidism. He could hear creation's song in every sound around him. In his heart, he could feel the peace of life and its ambient energy. He could absorb it, harness it, and fill his soul with it. If anyone with a wizarding eye could see, his soul's aura glowed an intense gold and green, crackling with power as he drew the power into himself.. And if someone had faith, they would see a wizard devout. In between meditative states of absorbing these energies, Kalero would finger his mother's Star of Galadrana and pray. Fastened around his neck by a leather thong, the medallion gave him hope. He hoped for the very power, the very same power denied by the Wizardrium.

Chapter 10

Rain beaded down on Sylvara's silver hair. Her griffin, Thamus, roared into the cumulonimbus of absolute black before them. Lightning cackled around her, but she held fast sensing the wind and steered her griffin onward within the clouds. She followed the constellation of the Great Boar, knowing that she held fast to the straight Eastern direction. Haste gave way to the wrecklessness of this flight, but Thamus pressed onward obeying her commands.

"Not much farther," she shouted, her voice shrouded by wind, rain, and thunder. The griffin screeched as eagles do, and sensed the fatigue of its rider. Thamus banked upward slightly, and felt a thermal gust take him into the storm. Having made this ride with her father, the griffin knew what to expect. The storm did not bother him.

Surrounding the Dwarven Mountains, a dense thick cloud of smoky clouds of lightning and storm. They were said to protect Dwarves of Krakmagoon from the unworthy. Barely awake and exhausted, the ceasing storm behind them and the new light of morning woke the half sleep Sylvara had achieved as she still instinctively held the reigns for dear life. Before her, the impressive mountain of Kragmagoon reaches its peak, the highest mountain in the chain of the Krakma Moutains. The peak had been flattened with numerous towers and circled stone platforms to dock the skybrigade galleons. Numerous stands of connecting tunnels and hollowed out mountains contained the jewel of the Dwarven Kingdom beneath its surface.

"There," Sylvara pointed. Her hand gesturing to one of the circles she knew to be the receiving dock for scheduled arrivals and attachés. Thamus darted down as if an eagle went for its fish beneath the waves. Dwarven guards screamed raising alarm. Sylvara's ride through the storm passed unnoticed by guards, galleon and wyvern patrol that circled constantly overhead.

When she landed, several winged and armored dwarves also landed simultaneously, each holding warhammers and axes contained by a chain to the gargoyle wings of their metal armor. She carried no weapon, and slid off Thamus with what grace nine hours of griffin flight would get you.

"I need to see King Thayumeer. It is a matter of life and death," she remained bowed to her dwarven guards.

"Who makes this request?" the dwarven Lieutenant asked still pointing his battle axe at the elf.

"I am Sylvara Quintoriel, Princess of Zalanthas. I am here to invoke the Treaty of Jaramasu."

Another guard eased his axe. "She came straight through that storm under our patrols."

"Then, she is worthy." The Lieutenant spoke. "Take her straightaway to King Thayumeer."

"Sir?" the young dwarf asked, knowing fully well the king would be attending to personal matters and family this early in the morning. He was young alongside his compatriot. Undoubtedly, they had never heard of the Treaty of Jaramasu, the mutual defense pact made long ago with Vanaxx Quintoriel and King Jaxon, the Hammer over two centuries ago.

"Nevermind, I'll take her myself," he bellowed. "Re-supply the galleons in dock immediately, and see to it they are crewed immediately. Make haste."

The two other dwarves eyed each other. "Those are unusual orders, sir."

"And I am Commander of the Watch in this hour, and I tell you to fuel up and make haste in crewing the warships in dock *in case they are needed*. We may be going to war."

When the young ones heard *war*, they took in the seriousness of their elder Lieutenant. They flew away on the wings of enchanted armor.

"Forgive them, Princess. They are young."

She staggered to her feet. "And you are?"

"Lieutenant Ibo, your majesty." He knelt into her as she staggered once more. "I assume that you do not wish to freshen up before seeing my lord." He eyed her soaked cape and riding boots.

"No. Make haste Lieutenant Ibo. Zalanthas will be under attack in two days time."

"Then, lean on me. We proceed directly into the Great Hall where Thayumeer and his family are eating."

Ibo escorted her inside, and they took the priority cart headed inside the city. Essentially, a square of smooth metal connected to a cable above and descended quickly into the main city of Krakmagoon below. Cut into the heart of the mountain, the city stood alit with the faint green glow of emerald litstone, a green eerie light produced by dwarven purification. The city stood in perpetual twilight. The buildings were marvelously sculpted stone. Statues of former kings, queens, and warriors stood as reliefs on the side of buildings as if they were living stone of jade, gold, and something like granite.

The priority transport into the city connected the Commander of the Watch to the Palace Garrison. Almost like an aqueduct, the track sloped down, but only slightly. As it descended, Ibo grabbed a torch, lit it, and signaled the garrison below. Though it took minutes to connect to the city garrison, already the forces below buzzed about like bees. "I signal for preparations of war. Do not be alarmed." He turned to her. "I hope you are as you say you are. Otherwise, I have given orders that make no sense and might land me in the stockade." Sylvara looked to the mountain city far below the forests of earth and mountain. She found it suffocating, but said nothing. She nodded and half-smiled. That seemed good enough for Lieutenant Ibo.

A bureaucrat met them below, Tendet Ysson. His face was beareded, scruffy, and bore a vexed face draped in the finest garments money could buy. "Why are our forces marshaling, lieutenant?"

"The Treaty of Jaramasu will be invoked in the hour," Ibo explained.

"By whom and for what?"

"By me, Princess Sylvara Quintoriel of Zalanthas. I must speak with Thayumeer."

Tendet grew annoyed. "You simply took her word on it?"

"I carry my father's seal as my own…"

Tendet cut her off. "Did it ever occur to you she could be an elven spy? An Allurian spy for that matter."

"She came through the storm. Our storms know she is worthy, so should you."

"Enough of this nonsense, Lieutenant. Give the order to calm down our forces at once." Tendet Ysson did not have the authority vested in the Commander of the Watch. For one shift, the Commander of the Watch could order the readiness of the entire kingdom's forces. Officially, Ibo was in command even as he swallowed hard. Tendet gestured for the Captain of the Garrison, and a retinue of officers approached taking their time. They bore the same annoyed looks.

Lieutenant Ibo still let the princess lean on him. He looked up at her. "Do you trust me?"

he whispered. "We'll get nowhere with these people." She smiled a devilish grin and nodded in silent agreement. Ibo had the same penchant for trouble. She instinctively wrapped her arms around him tighter, and tucked her one arm on the back where the chains of the battle axe connected to it on his back. He led her to the edge of the platform. Slowly at first, nobody noticed. Then, Tendet glanced back.

"Get back over here, Lieutenant Ibo."

"No," Ibo said. A determined and defiant face bore the determination of wings about to be spread. Ibo held on tightly to the elven princess. He jumped.

The air rushed passed them; the enchanted wings morphed outward. Ibo banked left and right flying wrecklessly through the palace corridors, towers, and outcropping of rocks and cavern gnawing teeth of stalactites above. He had only seconds, but timed it well. He dove straight for the balcony connected to the Great Hall. Ibo knew, as did the entire palace, the King took his meals there with his family after conducting state business. The enchanted marble of white with green and gold inlays became visible as Ibo and Sylvara approached the balcony. Palace alarms sounded their arrival, and King Thayumeer had come out on the balcony to observe the commotion. Ibo skidded on the floor before his king, and gently lowered Princess Sylvara still while kneeling as marble debris stretched for forty feet behind him. Thayumeer raised an eyebrow. Sirens blared and warning horns sounded in the distance.

"Sylvara?" Thayumeer said gasping in surprise.

"Thayumeer," she returned smiling at the awkwardly bold move of what she would take for the Skybridage's finest Skyknights.

"Jaramasu?" he asked.

"Jaramasu," she returned. "The Allurian Skyfleet makes for Zalanthas." Thayumeer stroked his beard contemplatively.

Lieutenant Ibo said nothing, but remained bowing. They both eyed him. "He helped me see you when nobody would admit me," she said in Dwarven. "Even now, your forces atop the mountain prepare their defenses and ready ships for possible war. He surmised that if the storm admitted me, so too should he admit me at once to see you."

"What is your name, Lieutenant?" King Thayumeer walked into the Great Hall and pulled his two war axes from over a mantle. He motioned for his wife and sons to depart.

"Ibo sire."

Flight of the Ravenhawk

"Rise anew, *Ibo the Ready*, Captain of the new Galleon Stormpasser in port." Ibo's face shined unsure what just happened. Sylvara sat down by the fire.

"There's no question I will fulfill my end of the Treaty of Jaramasu. Certainly, you'll explain it to me as we make haste."

Sylvara told him of Prince Kalero Tremayne, his brother, the reports from Lady Anarkana's well planned spy ring that kept tabs on the Allurian Empire and its recent slaughter of its own citizens of the Lightdweller faith. She told him of the impending attack and attempt on her life by the Allurian forces that called forth the skyfleet. At the end of it, Thayumeer suggested she sleep. The forces would be ready in three hours time.

Closing her eyes, Sylvara whispered silent prayers to the Ancestral Wood. She opened them and stared deeply into a goblet of red wine. She saw her face, and imagined seeing this crimson color shed in many of her kin.

Chapter 11

Towards the end of those two days, Kalero's meditation intensified in practice. Sweat saturated the leather thong, the small of his back and spine despite the coolness of the air near the waterfall. He shivered, his concentration lost as the mirroring reflection of water rippled in the wind.

Behind Kal and on the riverbank, Tao sat in full lotus. He, too, felt the nearby power, but only on an intuitive level honed by years of martial practice. Yet, his intuition was not as good as the wizarding eye. In fact, Tao sensed the two guards hidden in trees that watched his every move. There had been some suspicion of his motives, but Kalero's vouching for him had saved him a more horrible fate of interrogation by Anarkana's spies.

When nightfall fell, Tao opened his eyes. "It's almost time sire. Any longer and we risk being caught in the first assault on the city." He put on his shirt, and boots. "Do you think that ambient magick you've absorbed will nourish you long enough to wear the very armor that would drain it…and possibly kill you?" The words were hard to say.

Pushing himself up with his staff, Kal rose. "We'll have to see." Kal had to wear the armor when they entered the hangar.

Sighing, Tao did not like that one bit, not one bit at all. They walked together until they reached the recovered Skeeters. "You can fly this in the dark?" Kal asked.

"We'll have to see," Tao said smirking at the one known certainty of their plan. *Of course, he could.* Placing both hands at the ends of his staff, Kal pushed the staff at both ends. The staff shrank into what would pass for a small baton, and Kal dressed in the armor. Discomfort immediately settled in his bones, and he grimaced. Tao helped him put it on faster. The longer he wore, the shorter time he could actually live; the magickal alloys prevented and nullified magickal energy. Surround a wizard in the armor, and the wizard is magickally-suffocated, sapping his very life force.

With Tao's feet firmly planted, Tao switched the Skeeter on. A gibbous moon hung by a thread, and the stars, while still brilliant, faded in interspersed movements of moving cumulus. Nervously, Kal felt the suffocation begin, and held on tightly. In a second, the

177

humming insect wings came to life, and they were off. At first, Tao kept it low, bobbing in and out of ancient treetops.

"There," Tao pointed. Tao knew the approach patterns for the ships, keeping their approach low. Watching his prey, recon patrols buzzed about each destroyer on skeeters. When Tao and Kal broke the tree canopy, Tao saw them. Far above, massive white destroyers lined up in several stratified layers. The largest destroyer took point. On its aft, two landing crafts carried troops, which made up the bulk of the landing force. Behind them, four destroyers flew in a stacked formation, followed by three more support vehicles, which carried more troops and supplies. The troop carriers would be on high alert, and so it was now or never. "I'm going to try for a bottom one," Tao said pointing to the four destroyers in the group. The words bounced off Kal's ears; Kal merely concentrated on holding on.

If Tao kept too low and for too long without entering the right approach vector, then his motives would be known, and the mission would be over. If he fled the canopy too soon, he would be spotted, his motives known, and again, the mission would be over. He nodded to Kal, who by the look of him was not doing that well, but Kal had enough sense to give his thumbs-up. Biting his lip, Tao pulled back on the handlebar, and redirected the skeeter upward out of the canopy underneath Tao's target.

Above him, he saw another skeeter round the top. It would be only seconds until they came around again, or its opposite twin might. His foot clamped down, and accelerated the skeeter into rotation. Faster and faster, he flew. Then, he pulled back hard on the skeeter almost crashing into its underbelly. Both Tao and Kal felt the pressures of air and force almost turn everything black. Tao was quick though, and leveled out on the side parallel to the far side of the bulbous skyship near the aft under the lightning cannon.

Again, the skeeters came around, but Tao put his skeeter between them and the under cannon. It worked, and he had another chance, so he circled about coming from the underbelly riding close and fast to the underside and flipped straight into the open landing bay. He jammed hard on the breaks, and several guards looked on as the skeeter skidded on metal sending sparks to the side. One wing clipped onto the wall, the other singed and scraped along the hangar floor, and the onlookers heard the low hum of engine and power fade.

"Quickly, he needs help," Tao said. The alarmed men moved quickly to render aid. "Small arms fire. Elven poison probably." The two guards were Wizardslayers, and were by their comrade's side in seconds. "Help me get the armor off. Quickly." Each bore the insignia of Lord Tranek's men on their breastplate, a skull set into the crescent moon itself. In seconds, the men unclamped the fasteners of the enchanted armor. Putting his arms underneath Kal's head, Tao guarded the helm covering his face.

"Undo the waist and legs, I think that's where the wound is." Tao ordered in haste. Thinking it best to get them looking for what could not be found, the men worked diligently to save their comrade. As each part came off, Kal stirred a little bit more. Under the armor, the human wore a tunic of brown and matching leggings.

The first man rolled Kal over. "I don't see a wound." Lifting his head, he expected to see the pilot holding the head.

Squinting, the second said, "You know he looks an awful like…"

Stealthfully, Tao drew behind them. "I'm sorry" Tao severed their heads in one draw of the arcablade. Barely able to stand, Kal rose, still weak, and took off the helm. From the wall,

Tao grabbed a canister and broke the magick pink fuel over Kal. The magickal fuel absorbed quickly into his skin and covered his hair, and Kal felt his strength slowly return.

"Good thinking," Kal said. He went to the side of the skeeter, put on his pendant, and extended his staff. Looking at the corpses, Kal raised his hands and turned them invisible.

"Neat trick, Kal." Tao pushed the invisible bodies out of the hangar.

"That's nothing." Forming an image in his mind, Kal wove a glamour to conceal his person. Now, he looked twenty, a young lieutenant, non-descript in appearance, carrying a set of tools. Kal touched his finger to Tao's head. "When I'm ready, I'll contact your mind."

Tao nodded. "Set a delayed fire spell near those fuel canisters, too. Say, ten minutes." Kal nodded in return and cast it while Tao secured the room's only door. "Okay, now. I'll take the dorsal cannon. Make your way to the starboard cannon."

"Right," Kal said. His words felt odd. Could he do this? Could he go against that which he'd known his entire life? A part of him was reluctant to betray Alluria, but he moved— necessity giving way to conscience.

With nobody in sight, Kal went first into the corridor. Small light baubles casted an eerie red. The lights danced battle-ready on every floor. Footfalls echoed on callously cold metal. Nobody noticed a tinkerer looking about and inspecting various quarters, tubing, regulators, and levers, especially right before a battle. In truth, Kal went straight across, but had a little trouble finding the gunnery station. Before him, was a massive white structure with gold inlays stacked to a chair. In the chair, he saw an officer holding two controls. Extending out from the chair, golden energy, similar to the magickal fuel, rested in the middle under a gigantic crosshair. At the very tip, a large crystal was set fixed into a long shaft. Occasional tiny sparks emitted at its end as if barely able to contain the trigger-happy officer's need to destroy. During military operations, a gunner always manned the cannon, and until battle, the gunner kept the cannon rested at the ground while flying in formation with sister ships.

To his left, a younger officer, called the juicer, secured the racks of magickal canisters that could be exchanged for empty ones.

"Maintenance check," Kal said.

The slobbering officer with a portly belly, and thick eyebrows looked over the chair in surprise. "This close to a battle. Sorry lad. Can't not do." The juicer looked at him counting the negations of the previous sentence. Kal ignored it, the double-negative irking every part of his body.

"I apologize, but these orders come from King Darnashi personally. I'm to inspect every weapon and make sure that each one is in working order."

Shrugging, the juicer went to the corner and started reading a periodical of some variety. "Be quick, boy," the officer scoffed.

Putting two fingers together, Kal reassured himself. He didn't like it, but this mission was a necessity. He shot out a slicing wind of force. The gunner flew against the wall with a thud, which was absorbed by metal bulkheads and rivets; eyes widened in the juicer's face. His hands shook. Kal wasted no time. With a flick of his wrist, Kal webbed him in tendrils of thick strands. White and clear spider webs covered his mouth and body, and with a glance, Kal secured the door with magickal force behind it.

I'm ready down here, he sent to Tao.

****

Tao went up the stairs. Not wanting to give his identity up, he kept the visor down on his armor, and hastened his pace. He'd have to pass several of the quarters of the Wizardslayers who might know him, especially now since he betrayed King Darnashi personally. Against the wall, he grabbed a morphing lance, putting it between himself and anyone seeing his arcablades at his belt. He passed through undetected.

On a normal day, a fully-armored figure might draw suspicion, but since they were an invasion force, nobody took notice of fully-armored Wizardslayers walking through the decks, especially parts of the ship they would not normally travel. A Wizardslayer's presence would be perceived as the Wizardrium and the Crown's personal assurance to oversee the Allurian Skyfleet. The navy always despised their presence, and they gave them wide berth. While this situation worked to his advantage in getting to the dorsal cannon, two Wizardslayers brought a bottle of ale to share with the gunner upstairs. From the moment he walked in, Tao's signature weapons gave him away.

Tao looked down at the arcablades. "Shit," he said, and returned the gazes of the two fellow Wizardslayers.

The first shrugged; the second looked at the arcablades. "Yup," the second said.

Flight of the Ravenhawk

Tao lunged forward with the morphing lance, and it became a halberd. He caught the nose guard of the Wizardslayer holding his helm under one arm and the glass in the other. Twirling the halberd over his head, Tao struck down slicing into the visceral mass of the gunner parting the seat in two. Instantly, the second Wizardslayer activated his enchanted whip. A small runed handle emitted the blue glow similar to his arcablade, and with one snap, the energy lashed out and wrapped around the shaft of his arcablade where no magick alloy absorbed its energies. The able-bodied Wizardslayer yanked it clear out of his hands. Quickly, Tao drew the crescent dagger and threw it at the blood-soaked enemy that was readying his bracer crossbow; the spinning short sword found its mark while the first Wizardslayer holding the whip dove for cover. The crescent enchanted dagger floated in a perpetual circle where its victim's head had stood seconds ago.

Pushing the crescent dagger past his enemy's head, the Wizardslayer slashed again, but was painfully aware that he had two attackers—the crescent dagger behind him and the Ex-Commander Tao in front. Sidestepping the whip's lash and flash of blue, Tao rolled on the floor, and securely grasped his arcablade in a

crouched position. A slash came at him, and Tao
rose swatting the slash aside, and moved forward
only to find a slash across his advance halted
with the hissing blue energy strand whip before
him. In his hand, he attacked in a form more fluid
and certain fate of an enemy's death. Then, it hit.
A loud thud and presence filled his mind. *I'm
ready down here.*

In the same fluid motion, like an ocean
wave cracking a boulder, the blade swung and
sliced into the Wizardslayer's armor. Rather than
pull away and retreat with a wound in the torso,
the Wizardslayer hugged him with one arm, and
clenched the other in a fist held low. "Traitor," he
mouthed.

Click, click, two darts struck into the
armor. The dart punctured his lower gut ever so
slightly, but enough to seriously wound him. At
the presence of pain, Tao summoned the dagger
from behind, and jumped back towards the seat
of the cannon. *Ready down here, too,* Tao sent
through the telepathic connection.

****

Through the connection spell, the pain
of Tao's wounded abdomen filled Kal's mind.
Fire, Tao thought. With the four destroyers in the
body of the formation, the ASF Chesterton's
lightning cannons poured forth two steady

streams to the ASF Kasper and the ASF Tranek. The Kasper took a twenty-second stream arching along its ventral side underneath the fuel storage bins and the engines aft. On the starboard side, the Tranek took a hit directly at the engineering section for the same amount of time. Neither ship suspected that the Chesterton would fire in stacked formation. Now, the Allurian Skyfleet alarm sounded, screaming through every hallway. The other ships ordered their wizards to divert cannon power to energy shield spells. Both the Kasper and the Tranek lost control, a bellowing smoke trail from above meant that the ship above was crashing down hard now into the heart of the ancestral wood.

On the bridge, Captain Rapa took the helm, and pulled back hard on the ship's wheel. Levers gave, and the stress on the ship's rivets sounded. Pipes exploded, and the Chesterton buckled under strain of her quick-thinking captain. Rapa banked upward hoping to climb to the side as the Kasper came directly down. He screamed for the cannons to be secured, and flicked on the all hands-on deck lights in the decks below. Everyone on the ship saw their possessions float almost backward as the Chesterton climbed. Then, it buckled again.

J. Edward Hackett

An explosion ruptured the underbelly. The delayed fire spell ignited intensely. The skeeter bay's fuel depot ran along the central ventral lines that fed the Chesterton's magickal furnaces and engine. Without thinking, Captain Rapa ordered the evacuation, and the red lights flashed. Time to go.

Chapter 12

Throughout the struggle, Kal made his way up the stairs, he could feel Tao's presence. The ship's crew hastily ran around trying to figure out what happened, and unlike the duel with his brother, everything slowed—the explosion whining in his ears. He felt the psychic urgency on the ship. A pink fire and smoke filled the hallways, dissipating magickal fumes into the air. To Kal, these fumes gave him more power, intoxicating the air. Kal felt almost giddy with power. He needed it, yearned for it, and consumed it. A rush filled him, a rush he at first did not like, but reveled in nonetheless.

The power surged through him, and for the first time he understood the Allurian way, the way just one spellcaster could alter the fate of war itself and why power of magick and ego were parallel. The Allurians regarded them as one thing, and while he knew differently, Kal found sympathy with that hubris. Magickal power was addictive for the undisciplined. The addiction was not knowing where one's will in magick and one's actual station in the empire stopped. The equivocation of power – magickal and political – stood for both ability and station.

Dropping to the pool of blood surrounding Tao, Kal secured Tao's swords and put his one arm around the young man. In the descent, time slowed. From the cracked window and damaged wall Kal saw the other ship, the Tranek, far off in the distance, crash into the forest. A half-mile of the ancestral wood was devoured and uprooted by the monstrous machine, which had cracked in two. Behind him, navy personnel and Wizardslayers burst into the room. With some coaxing, Tao stood, and Kal dropped the illusion of his person.

"You!" the Lieutenant screamed, encompassing both Kal and Tao in one curse of condemnation. Kal returned the shocking look, and gestured nervously. Kal needed a few more seconds so he sent a wind spell at the Lieutenant and his men sending them tumbling down the corridor. He shot the same web spell over Tao's bleeding torso. "That'll have to do for now."

When the Lieutenant emerged once more, he peered into the room from the door. In a flurry of magical power Kal and Tao morphed into sand in the wind. The wind-sand whirled around the room searching for a hole in the ship.

Flight of the Ravenhawk

When it finally found one, it slowly leaked out—
the perfect escape for a Wizard.

Chapter 13

On the spell-raised walls of Zalanthas, and specifically in the tower facing the fleet, King Vanaxx wore leather armor, plated with ironwood leaves and a helm that sported the antlers of his crown. He surveyed the fleet with the magnifying lens. In the distance, three ships went down in succession and the skeeters launched like a hornet nest come to life. Their mechanized contraptions like locusts set upon a field blocking any definitive view of the destroyers and personnel carriers. The fleet separated randomly rather than clustering together in strict formation, which would make things difficult. The two personnel carriers still remained, and two destroyers hung back along with the frigates in tow, yet they still approached, more slowly than before.

More than likely, their commanders were meeting again, deciding on an alternative war plan. With the sudden loss of several skyfleet destroyers, Kal bought them time. King Vanaxx ordered more scattered deployment should those skyfleet ships attempt another run. Ecomancers morphed wood and plant adding cover and camouflage to towered defenses.

Vanaxx raised his scepter and pointed to several soldiers that bore a different standard than the rest. They blew their horn distinct from the others on the opposite side. From behind him on the many platforms, trees, and entrances to the Underrealm, wooden statues of griffins came alive all at once. They would make their way on the canopy floor, surprising the invasion force from below. Horn blasts mobilized the elven guard, and they all ran hopping from tree branches to the forest floor and over the wall.

The griffins, half-eagle and half-lion sprinted forward into battle. Their riders secured in place by thick leather saddles around the lion-torso. Their ferocity shook the earth, as they charged toward the enemy. Yet that ferocity stood silenced by the mechanistic forces in the sky above.

In the distance, the remaining destroyers, the ASF Ebon Hawk and the ASF Hammer fell in behind each other, and they directed their lightning cannons to the forest floor below. Strafing runs. Lightning tore earth and forest in massive blows of magickal force, dispersing massive sections of trees and growth below, and each fired indiscriminately while circling back, each moving opposite of the other in giant arches before coming together in formation again where they started. Black smoke floated into the sky as the conflagration grew in the wake of the lightning cannons. Thunder clapped as the air expanded quickly as the flashes of the cannons erupted in the canopy below. They were making clearings.

Suddenly, the hornet nest of Wizardslayers advanced beyond the circles, and following upon their heels of the skeeters, the personnel carriers landed swiftly, one partially damaged as the elves shot their own cannons from the spell-raised towers. Metal ramps clamped down on the scorched earth, and horsemen, cannons, and debris-clearing tank vehicles rolled onto the forest floor sooner than the griffins could arrive.

What Vanaxx did not see was General Litner's modified plan. He'd sent only thirty percent of his skeeters towards the city. His scarred face and balding head peered out atop the Ebon Hawk, waiting. A snicker of delighted appeared, and an internal sense of pride poured from his confident eyes. He wore solid black plate, and carried no weapon that could be seen. When the intensely thick cloud of skeeters passed overhead, the overzealous griffin-riders shot arrows and launched from the canopy into the thick of battle, their location revealed. The mass of skeeters flew in cloud cover above. A mechanical horn sounded, and they dove. Each carried three large balls of magickal explosives. Each bomb could take down sections of wall, Litner ordered that each skeeter used one on where they estimated the griffin riders lurked below. It worked to devastating effect.

Far below, the griffin-riders started to climb. Then, explosions surrounded them at the level of the canopy. Wooden splinters and trees came down as intense balls of destruction and heat evaporated everything they touched. Burnt bodies and wood permeated the air. Still, the griffin-riders fought valiantly overtaking some in the first wave, but their numbers could no longer be effective. Vanaxx committed ninety-percent of his forces. When the explosions cleared, griffin-riders and skeeters exchanged arrows and blue bolts fired from the lances affixed to the mechanical arm of the skeeters. While outnumbered, the elven archers found their marks more often than the Wizardslayer. It did not matter.

Looking through the magnifying lens, King Vanaxx swallowed hard. The Ebon Hawk and the Hammer lurked just beyond the clutches of the forward towers lightning cannons and projected their shield cover to deflect bombardment from the towers. Their shields extended underneath them as smaller troop carriers landed in the clearings of flame and wood. In the distance, Vanaxx could hear the mechanized sounds of the Allurian war machines, and he knew that like many kingdoms before his own, he felt the same dread as those that fell to the Allurian legacy.

He could not think that way now. Vanaxx ordered his flag bearers to communicate retreat to all his forces. Before him, the remaining griffin-riders and elven archers fled back to the city walls. Some skeeters engaged them, but the bulk remained behind just before the shields. Their primary mission had been to guard the clearing from any interference. Vanaxx ordered the towers to fire at will, a different groups of horns sounded, and the air seared with the intense energies of lightning cannons. Tanks, siege platforms on mechanized vehicles, horses, and footman trekked through the forest out of range, but encroached. Spreading thin and fanning out their approach, the Allurian forces made for difficult targets. Withdrawing to the wall, the remaining elven forces on the perimeter retreated backward. With their dead around them, they fell back to the wall. Within the city, human boys and men took up sword and bow, even if reluctant and untrained. Before them, the Allurian forces gathered on a ridgeline.

It looked bleak. Even more so when, beside the tower, a maelstrom of sand and sorcery came together and formed a bleeding Tao and Kal. "Healers, I need a healer. Now!" Kal shouted. Several arrived and immediately carried Tao off.

"Are you injured, Prince Kalero?" a healer asked, gesturing to Kal's blood soaked robes. Kal shook his head once.

"Take care of Tao," Kal instructed and climbed the stairs to meet beside King Vanaxx.

"How do we fair?" he asked the king.

"Not good, I'm afraid." Vanaxx gestured to the occupational line. "They devastated our griffin riders. I was a fool, and now Zalanthas will pay the price."

"I'll talk to them," Kal said. "First things, first."

Feeling the ley lines nearby, he drew strength and opened his heart once more to the beating pulse of creation. One heartbeat, one pulse, one raindrop—that's all he needed, and he dare not take any more than that. Balance, creation's ebb and flow, surrounded this place and took form amongst the living and dead things of the forest, earth, and sky. Kal tasted the power and washed away the destruction of what transpired before. The battle's recent dead lingered in the memory of his burdened heart, yet he pushed past that by listening now to the Source. He listened to the earth, and with the thousand pounding footfalls of anticipated battle. The Source spoke to him directly; it gave the true name of *earth* and the deep *roots* that carved the Underrealm far below. The will of the Source came over him. Both will and power merged in his mind to a height never before felt. Kal became vessel to that power, and while it had no personality, he could feel it building in him like the avalanche about to fall. In that instant, Kal knew what he could do.

Closing his eyes, he changed the shape of his dress. His white robes became a breastplate adorned with the ravenhawk banner and coat of arms chosen long ago at his ascension into manhood. Though trivial, the ravenhawk had become a symbol; his symbol, and now one of sheer defiance. First in flight, but now landing before them here. Magick entered the staff, and it, too, changed into a high flag bearing the same standard. Standing on the wall, a small bauble of light and energy formed around Kal. He floated off the wall and moved to hover halfway between the ironwood wall and the amassing forces of Alluria before him. As he floated, he drew strength from all ley lines, a gift to create balance, and the power appeared translucent and blue for all to see. The magick tasted primal and sweet like ancient sap ready to burst forth on a thousand-year tree. Ribbons of energy surged around Kal's body. In drawing this much power and ambient mana, the magick became visible for all. Minor wizards on the other side looked on stupefied, their controlling efforts incapable of channeling what the Ancestral Wood gave to Kal. All sensitive to magick could feel Kal's channeling of unseen forces like the dry stillness before a storm. Kal muttered silent words of the spidery language of magick, his voice began to boom and vibrate the metal of armored-plated men in the army before him.

"Allurians of Venda. You've come to wage war against a peace-seeking nation at the request of my brother. You've come for me, really. I am here. Your battle is with me! Is it not? Yet, I ask you just one simple question. Decide as you must. I am defender, now, of these people. Many of your fellow citizens are behind this wall, massacred perhaps by some of you here, and my brother. They raise sword against you

since you pose risk to their families and friends.
I am Prince Kalero, heir to Hiraeus's throne. I
stand before you as your future king. Those that
lay down their swords today will be given
amnesty.

The forces across the way burst out into
laughter. Allurian pride bellowed in their
stomachs. They were winning, and their enemy
threatened them alone.

"So now, the question: Do you seek
peace with those behind this wall and me, or do
you raise arms against Kalero the Just? Do you
do my brother's bidding? Do you support a
tyrant? Condone the slaughtering of innocents?
Do you serve a man consumed by power and who
practices necromancy and the dark arts. Chose
now, but be warned. If you persist in attacking
these people on this day, I will destroy you as I
destroyed your skyfleet destroyers.

"Chose now, Allurians. Ravenhawk or
Dragon."

Across the way, people shuffled
discussing with whom they should join, support,
and some backed away throwing down arms.
Vanaxx bowed at the wall, and every elf and man
followed suit. Kal never turned his back on the
Allurians on the ridge. Even far above, General
Litner smirked at the audacity of whom he

wished to serve. He hung on those words, but knew his duty.

Clicking a switch with a crystal suspended in a handle fixed to a circle, Litner spoke into the microphone. "Proceed with the attack, Commander."

The tanks sounded their horns. Tank wheels crunched on wood and gears spun. The attackers continued without hesitation. Kalero Tremayne stabbed the standard-staff into the ground, and from his person, a white field of magickal energy poured forth.

In unison, the tanks, cannon gunners, Wizardslayers, and archers set their crosshairs upon Kal. But Kal's strength held; his spells and power fueled by the gifted energies of the ancestral wood and the Source itself. Arrow, cannon, spell wind, fire, ice, and lightning cannons from above—all bounced off the forcefield. And still they came at him. Some in the distance stared in wonder.

General Litner slumped in his chair. "Approach at half-speed. Gunners fire at will." Like judgment from heaven, lightning bolts streamed into the white shield, yet Kalero sat in a full-lotus position hovering in the air as the shield encompassed him and the city at his back. For several minutes, Kal floated, meeting chaos with peace, motion with stillness. Eventually, the fighting ceased though the cannons continued to fire. No sign of fatigue nor a drop of sweat signaled an end to Kal's power. Kal simply hovered there, floating like a lotus held in suspension by the wind itself.

Kal's power glowed the same fiery white in his eyes as the absorbing forcefield protecting the city. His voice echoed. "Since you've chosen the dragon, you will die," his voice boomed, yet his voice was not entirely his own. A tinge of reverberation and echo resonated with the power funneling to him. He had become like the floodgate letting forth a great flood. Some ran retreating back into the distance, and the utterly stupid tried penetrating the shield physically; they were thrown into the air as the shield blocked both magickal and physical attacks.

Kal did nothing the forest was not willing to do. Instead his power unified the disparate wills of plant, tree, animal, stream, rock, and the roots of the world-tree, the true essence of the Ancestral Wood. All trees were connected, running deep into the Underrealm, fueling one will and one massive node that Kal's power tapped into to fuel these effects. Like the trees, all nodes, he felt, were connected. His will and thought touched every living thing in the ancestral wood. He could feel every emotion of the forest's inhabitants. The elder trees were angry, angry at the surface world for tearing asunder their green children. In his meditative state, the tree song became louder like a thousand roars of thunder stirring the heavens at once. He surrendered his will to the stream of life, and its Source. Underneath, the earth swelled at Kal's command ready and waiting for him to unleash fury.

The Allurians looked at Prince Kalero; they were unsure what to do. His power had stopped them dead in their tracks. Kal gave them a chance he knew they would not take. He never lied to them. If they remained, then they would be destroyed, and he'd given word to the residents inside Zalanthas that he would protect them. His word was his bond both to the past and to his future. The Allurians and the Zalanthians were at a stand still between judgement and time. Then, in two heartbeats and an exhale, four soldiers placed their swords at his feet outside the shield. They got on their knees lowering themselves before the floating prince. Soon, six others followed suit. They chose peace, and threw their swords down on the ground. Ten in all, they bowed, and then more came.

"Enough!" the Commander screamed. "Pick up those swords, or die." Those soldiers did not move, but kept their heads bowed. Arrows flew at them. Several flinched, and the shield lashed out extending itself to encompass the redemption of ten.

"Wrong answer," Kal said in his unearthly voice.

Inside his being and underneath the Allurians, the earth, stones, pebbles, rocks of granite, sediment and roots stretched. The roots called loudly to his soul. In Kal's mind, he heard the true names for all the pieces of creation woven together like a fabric. His silent will, a mage of thought, pull at those seams. He listened to their screams far below his feet, their agony, and he could feel the rage of oak, ash, cedar, and other trees he could not recognize, but their endless age could be felt. They whispered their names to him. The Allurians threatened the Ancestral Wood itself, and the forest's children, their elven children who had sought the balance with the very life around them. The power here was primordial and unnervingly so, but embraced aspects of harmony Kal regarded as the Source. As the wind blew into the trees, the leaves sang their song, the pain carrying on every note, and as Kal's power extended into the forest

Flight of the Ravenhawk

Vanaxx could hear it, feel it, and almost touch it. Kal's will surrendered to the forest and life itself. In this very moment, his power was not his own. Kal touched his fingers together folded into a triangle as both index fingers came together. His power found unity there, his will and thoughts now one with the tree root. For several moments, the tree roots transmuted and morphed below, yet no power shook the earth to give warning. Kal was done with warnings.

In one heartbeat, the earth shook and split open, swallowing the forces on the ridgeline. Allurian troops fell into an endless chasm as the earth jutted up from behind. Screams of the fallen trailed off into silence. The earth curled under the Allurians forcing them into the maw, even as they fled. Kalero parted his hands and extended them in a waving gesture. The earth rolled like a blanket unfurled flinging tanks and siege platforms tumbling after their fallen soldiers. Kalero let chaos reign for a moment, and then, Kalero snapped his hands back, and the earth rolled back. Several troops climbed trees, and the trees fell willingly. Wizardslayers carried fallen troops to safety, and Kalero let them go.

From the bridge, General Litner shook at his power. He overheard the navigator.

"That's…that's impossible." Litner just witnessed the earth swallow his men. All of his forces dead in one instant.

Litner's tactical officers, one of which was Mageborne, became pale. He too whispered in utter shock. "Nobody has that much power."

Below, Kal collapsed. Even though the power surged into him, the channeling took its toll on him. The ten soldiers who laid arms at his feet carried him back to the wall and the gates parted letting them in. Kal's staff flapped behind them, the shield spell still shimmering, and as Kal's consciousness went dark, so did his shield spell cease shimmering for the terror that awaited. However, now, they stood a more equal chance of defeating the Allurians.

In his breast, Litner knew what was right. It tugged at him, but fear drowned his mind. Kal's pronouncement against his brother was correct, and he'd answer to the Prime Magus and King Darnashi if he failed. The remaining support ships pulled in behind him as he barked orders to the command staff on the bridge. "Attack pattern, Tranek!" The Ebon Hawk turned toward the city, the hornet's nest of skeeters regrouped for strafing runs. The bombs dropped on the wall first. Elven archers fired at will as enchanted arrows burned white hot. Flashes of light and explosions ripped the wall to pieces, but so did skeeters erupt in explosions. Remaining griffin-riders launched from the reserves pushing back some of the advance in a glorious battle of equals.

Then, the wall fell despite their best efforts.

"To the trees!" Vanaxx snapped.

Vanaxx's honor guard fell in behind the ten men carrying Kal's body, the mage exhausted from the surging convergence of power bestowed to him by powers beyond in the Source and Node. They jumped. The honor guard heard a crack from Kal's ribs. Molten rock exploded as lightning cackled from the ships far away. More conventional cannon fire erupted around them. How had they survived the day thus far? It was anyone's guess. In haste, they made it to the evacuation elevator, a guardsman cut the line that sent the elevator hurling the King's guard back into the forest, Kal, and the Redemptive Ten soldiers to the upper platforms of the city. Arrows flew. Several skeeters witnessed the retreat and gained on them. It seemed like an end. Another part of Zalanthas's wall fell, though it did no good to the Allurian forces on the ground. Kal had made sure no force occupied the city with the defeat of the ridgeline. General Litner weakened in his tactical position advanced with everything he had, and without the two lightning towers keeping them at bay or powering a shield, it was only a matter of time until the fate of Zalanthas was decided on by the generosity of an Allurian conqueror, a waning spell, and airship bombardment. The reckless elevator hinged on the upward platform as archers exchanged blasts with the pursuing skeeter. Kal stirred recognizing the danger.

Twisting his fingers, vines stretched out from the treetops. Their massive wooden fibers stretched out with solid oaken hands grabbing the advancing skeeter. The sudden stop hurled the driver from the seat sending him forward and falling to his death. Kal motioned to be put down. The honor guards obliged and his look of resignation at their situation grew sour.

"Why the long face Kal?" the King asked.

"Sarcasm is not becoming of you," Kal grinned. He felt the fractured rib from the unconscious carry. "That bad, huh?"

"Yes."

Then, one of the honor guard spotted black specks in the distance. Holding his side, Kal rose to see the distant specks in the East. "Oh no, airships." His words were an unconscious reflex, but from his periphery, King Vanaxx resigned himself to the fate of impending death. Had the Allurians split their forces? And then everything went black for Kal.

Chapter 14

Sylvara kicked her heels into the griffin. She wore riding goggles common to the Dwarven Skybrigade. She clicked the side as additional lenses fell over the dominant eye, and magnified faraway images. Beside her, the smaller faster ships, old galleons modified, or skyrigged as it was called, fell in behind her. "Faster Thamus. Faster." A thunderous "Kaw" from the griffin emanated the fear, desperation, and fury of its rider. Thamus sensed these things stirring in her master's throat. In the distance, Sylvara saw the damage. Smoke and fire burnt the Ancestral Wood far below. Two towers had already fallen. She swallowed hard. Her father's tower lay in ruins. Parts of the wall were breached where the towers stood, and she saw elves dying, falling, and fighting, behind a partial protection spell still blocking one entrance into the city, but it, too, was failing. The elves gave no quarter to the advancing Allurian Skyfleet, but their time was limited to how effective they could be against them.

Flight of the Ravenhawk

Facing King Thayumeer, she nodded a determined look after a second "KAW!" from Thamus. King Thayumeer bellowed orders in his white armor, lined and streamed in blue. On his back, sharp-axe wings tapered to bat-like segments. In his hand, he held two war axes with magickal chains that held them secure in his armor's bracers. Standing tall on the raised ship platform as it fell through the air, Thayumeer jumped. Dwarves wearing the same armor rode atop Wyverns and flew through the sky in abundant number like the Allurian skeeters in the distance. Hiding behind the flying galleons, they parted, flying more freely. From the port side, a cargo door slid open. Similarly armored figures jumped onto the wing's edge and took flight in the midday sun.

****

"Dwarves!" Vanaxx screamed. "Sylvara has brought Thayumeer's aid." Kal found himself beside Tao. Several elven guards took cover behind the door, but he heard the screams. Rising a little, he saw out the window, and flying galleons hurled cannons. The skeeters pressed on with their assault, though now they regrouped focusing on the more pressing threat of the Dwarven Skybrigade.

211

In the distance, Sylvara saw elves dying, falling, and fighting. The archers concealed themselves in the tree city. They were harder to kill here; their guerilla tactics honed by centuries of practice. This was not Zalanthas's first fight.

****

Litner's fist smashed hard on the console. *How had dwarves come to their aid?* Uniformed officers nervously watched the general. They knew what was coming. General Litner took the crystal microphone, switched the dial, and placed it in front of him.

"King Darnashi, Lord of Alluria."

In the blue light, King Darnashi's face appeared. The entire bridge saw his demonic face of skeleton and fused flesh-metal face and that burning necromantic eye. The general regained his composure, putting his hands behind him, and bowed his head.

"Rise and report, General."

"We've lost half the fleet and the main invading force. The Dwarven Skybrigade has just arrived to aid the Elves. We could lose the Ebon Hawk and the Hammer to their wyverns and galleons. I advise retreating."

Darnashi eyed Litner skeptically. "And what about the rest of the fleet, General Litner?"

"Destroyed, my lord. By your brother."

"My brother spellbound three destroyers? Even for him that's unlikely," King Darnashi spat. His skepticism was tinged with jealousy.

"Your treacherous brother snuck aboard with the traitor, Commander Tao. They commandeered lightning cannons, fired at ships in formation, and sabotaged our attack."

"My brother," Darnashi said. He could find no words to express his frustration.

"Your brother swallowed the landing force in the earth. He opened up a chasm right below their feet. We have no forces to occupy the city even if we could get past his enchantments, the dwarven fleet, and the remaining elven forces."

Standing above the mirror, Darnashi's face loomed like a specter now, an imperial ghost. He rose in the throne room staring down at the communication device. "Make for Venda. Full retreat General." Litner heard his disdain. "I'll deal with you when you arrive." Litner ordered the change of course, and the Allurian ships pulled back. The bridge crew bowed their heads. General Litner was as good as dead just like the ground forces buried alive. By day's end, the elven forest patrols would have killed the remaining ground forces.

****

Atop the Gathering Oak, many attended the meeting. Commanders of both Elven and Dwarven stripes attended, and Vanaxx ordered that it take place in Common. The Vendan humans had nominated Brother Whiskers and Dorn to represent them. The Gathering Oak had been an ancient tree in which a stadium of seats had been built. Each layer atop the tree encircled along a ring, and it got smaller and smaller as one proceeded to the bottom level where the War Council sat with all eyes on them. In the sky above them and in new day's light, a beautiful early dawn settled into calm azure sky. As the highest tree in Zalanthas, one could climb it and see the rest of the many thousands of miles of Ancestral Realm before them. At the top today, some mourned for the loss of life and balance as the unnatural fires still burnt in the distance, a deathly reminder of yesterday's events.

Thayumeer ordered two wyverns in the sky to have around the clock patrols. Some of the armored dwarves rode in saddles of shimmering metal and mail on top of the legless wyverns that soared above. "Your will is our command," his men said. Vanaxx and Thayumeer embraced as old friends before the assembled throngs of people, and Sylvara hugged her father.

"I did not think that she'd get to you in time," Vanaxx said.

"Aye, she did." He gestured to the wyverns resting and finally to her. "She rides with a Fury's rage." The remaining wyverns coiled themselves in the strong trees, or used their ice breath to put out fires in the forest and within the elven city.

"Where's Kal?" she asked.

Vanaxx smirked. "Behind you."

Behind her, Kal hobbled on a crutch, his torso wrapped in bandages. He bowed as best he could. Thayumeer greeted him by pounding his heart, a sign of informal respect amongst the Dwarven people.

"This must be Prince Kalero," Thayumeer said, twisting his knotted, fire-red beard into even tighter knots. His lips formed a thin line.

"He is," Vanaxx said. Vanaxx extended his arms and corralled them to the table. " Sorry, there's not more time for introductions. We've got much to discuss. And every moment I make my lords wait, the more nervous they grow." At the sight of Sylvara, Kal hung back a little. He waved awkwardly as if to say "We're still alive."

Sylvara hugged him. "The entire city saw you. They said you stopped the invaders."

He said nothing for a minute. Then, he smirked. "More like the roots and earth asked me to stop them. My power is not my own often."

She held him tightly. "You listened like a druid."

"Just as you instructed." They both looked in the direction of the circled table where everyone gathered. These deliberations were open to everyone though whatever decision king and lords arrived at would be respected by all above.

"Any advice for politics?" he asked.

"You're a prince. You should know how this works," she said, trotting off in the direction gathering table.

"Yeah, but I'm not very good at it," he muttered under his breath. As she went farther ahead, Kal took his pendant in hand. "If I were good at politics, then others wouldn't need to die in my pursuit of it. By the Source, I must put an end to it." His words met the air and soon dissolved into the emptiness that ate away inside.

Shurdanatos, Anarkana, Thayumeer, Vanaxx, Sylvara, and Prince Kalero sat around an enchanted table that mapped the contours of the land morphed out of the bark. Vanaxx spun it to resemble their topography, and the relief morphed indicating positions of the former towers, wall, scorched earth, the ancestral wood, and the wreckage of the three destroyers in relation to Zalanthas and Venda.

"Where is Lord Vetranalaa?" Shurdanatos asked.

Anarkana embraced him with uncanny grace, and the elven lord fell silent. "My...my friend."

His eyes were now red. Rage and anger filled his mind. In his loss, he pointed to Prince Kalero, "This is your fault. You hear me? Your fault!"

Kal slunk back unsure of himself.

"Enough!" Vanaxx hissed. "I am to blame. I gave Prince Kalero sanctuary and lest you forget he saved us. A lot more would have died yesterday." The rebuke was enough to silence Vetranalaa's whispers. "We must form a pact here and now. The three races here: dwarf, elf, and human."

"There hasn't been a War Council in six centuries. If you recall old friend, the Allurians founded their nation in that last war," Anarkana said.

Thayumeer rubbed his beard contemplatively, the braids almost falling out as

217

J. Edward Hackett

he stroked it. "Aye, it's been a long time since the steel of the Eastern Mountains had purpose beyond the forge. We stand with our elven kin, but I fear a prolonged war is out of the question. Our resources are limited. We are here for treaties long ago signed and blood oaths taken. We care little for the fate of humans. We are here for our elven brothers and sisters."

"The real question is: How does this end?" Sylvara asked.

"With me defeating my brother," Kal said. "When I defeat him, Alluria will open its borders, peacefully trade with everyone here, and we'll share our knowledge of the High Art Magick with everyone." Thayumeer's eyes widened at the prospect. Many of the dwarven wizards departed to learn more than the elemental arts of morphing earth and stone. For the Allurians were a pragmatic people accepting anyone who excelled at the High Art. For them, magick was power, and worth more than any gold. Entire trade deals with the Allurians may have rested on acquiring rare volumes from the libraries of the many races.

Anarkana scoffed. "Insolent boy," she said in Elven.

"Do you doubt me!" Kal hissed in perfect elven.

"Enough" both Vanaxx and Sylvara said in unison.

Anarkana faced away from Kal. Anarkana glanced back quickly. "Can you finally do it, Magelord? Can you kill your own kin?" Anarkana asked. They all faced him. For the first time in his life, Kal fiercely meant it. "Yes, I'll kill my brother. Get me into the city unnoticed, and he'll pay for everything. Everything."

Sylvara glanced at Anarkana. "Perhaps, it's time to use that spy network of yours for something more than information."

"Then, it's settled," Vanaxx said. "We take the fight to the Allurians and put Kal on the throne. Once that's done, this war can be done."

"I'd have his word on it, a spelloath with the price of death. That is, should he fail?" Shurdanatos declared. The words were like bitter steel pulled from the forge. Those words hung in the air radiating heat for all who listened.

Vanaxx and Sylvara exchanged looks of apprehension. Kalero raised his palm. There was no reluctance in him, but the passionate abruptness of unsettled rage. Sylvara shook her head silently, but he ignored her warning. "I'll do it." He folded both hands into each other and bowed to Shurdanatos who was still lost in his own grief over his friend, but he recognized Kal's willingness.

"Should we all not pledge our deaths to the defeat of King Darnashi?" Sylvara asked.

"She's got a point old friend," Anarkana said, holding Shurdanatos arm reassuringly. He nodded his head.

"Yes…yes. That's the first thing we do."

"Aye, a spelloath, then!" Thayumeer exclaimed, and he guzzled more ale at the promise of allies and battle.

"My dear?" Vanaxx said. Sylvara was the only druid present, and so she drew out her dagger. For some time, the room was silent. Sylvara let the light of the day's sun glint off the knife until it glowed a distinct blue. Druids drew strength from nature's life energy. But as Kal learned, the power did not come when called nor was it controlled by the wizard. It came when it was ready, in its own time whereas by contrast Wizards imposed their will upon the tapestry of creation. Sylvara composed the spell oath in her mind, asking nature to listen.

"Before the Light, before Queen's knowledge and scepter's might, we hold these promises dear in our fight. Each here will sincerely seek Darnashi's end; For this we live, with all purposes amend. To not do as yee will promise on this night shall lead to death's invite. Let those who support Darnashi's life, know our strife. As long as he lives, the three races will unite. One front for one death, one treaty to draw last breath. On this I swear!" The knife shone an otherworldly blue. Kal took the knife and pricked his finger on the blade. The knife flared once and absorbed his blood. Thayumeer took the knife next and pricked his thumb. Shurdanatos, Anarkana, and Vanaxx followed suit. Like the Allurians who had every race and prominent mageborne family in its city, the three races united under one banner.

Chapter 15

As the male personality and incorporeal demon, Witness did not usually possess female bodies. Such a possession felt odd as humans referred to him as "her", yet under the pseudonym Irina Corovan, his inner mind delighted in the refugee's caravan of pain. Witness fed on the resonance of that psychic pain as it ebbed and flowed like tide in an ocean. On the outskirts of Venda, several towns had taken liberty with the royal edict against the Lightdwellers. Some merely forced them out of homes, running them to the outskirts of the towns and into the countryside. Others burned them channeling their own inner turmoil and scapegoating the Lightdwellers on stakes or inside their homes for the oppression of the crown. Wooden temples toppled to the ground by hordes of the unenlightened and torches alike— sometimes with bodies in them. As the chaos continued, more Lightdwellers fled and found the underground railroad of refugees sludging through the forest. As the caravan went, the amount of refugees accrued in number like a snowball becoming an avalanche by the end. The caravan could no longer mask its true purpose, but at the moment, nobody pursued them, and Witness knew why. She was to learn more and report back to her master. The Prime Magus kept the scouts at a distance.

Soon, Irina Corovan learned that the elves had supported the underground railroad of safe havens, and supply caches along the route. Established long ago by tactically adroit elves, these routes snaked from the Allurian capital into the Ancestral Wood itself. At times, the devotion and charity of the Lightdwellers made him sick. As Witness fed and sustained his form on the misery and trauma of the victims, so too did the Lightdweller faith and celebration of prayer bring him great pain. The Lightdwellers served as a continual reminder of the light in Witness's eyes, but more practically, it was a conduit of information. A spy network set up in the Allurian's backyard now blatantly exposed by the exigency of those around him. Each stop only knew two ahead of it, and sometimes only one. Witness sensed the glamour of the humble humans that saw to the safety of the Lightdwellers. They were actually elves, and they cleverly helped all Lightdwellers passing themselves off as mere farmers whose cabin in the clearing grew tremendous amounts of food. Witness suspected some of their motives were genuine. These glamours were prepared elsewhere before their mission, and he felt free to move about them when the caravan camped.

Irina had a small fortune when "she" left, but now only a third remained. Witness won a place and favor with the whole caravan. Witness-turned-into-Irina bribed townsfolk to turn away, and even negotiated large purchases of food. "For the faith" was all Witness could say. That's all he could stomach, and as a noble woman, the commoners gave Witness-turned-into-Irina wide berth. At least, Witness looked noble, even if Witness wasn't. People looked up at *Irina* in admiration, not fear. Though keeping up appearances of nobility and self-sacrifice, Witness did not like being admired. Fear guaranteed results; admiration garnered nothing but indebted respect to which no agony came and from which he could not feed. Sulking along the miserable road of mortals is hard enough, even harder when Witness felt the power of their faith linger in the air at times like moisture before a storm.

The power of faith burned Witness, swelling and churning his insides. Sometimes, it burned intensely. Other times it was weak like a sunburn scalding his spiritual being, and in these moments of agony Witness-turned-into-Irina had to be nice—nice and admired? Being spellbound to the Prime Magus made it easier. The binding of his will gave some measure of protection; it hurt more to turn away from his purpose, and so Witness drew strength to be nice back to them. If zealous villagers attacked, the carnage would be lovely, even deserved. An attack might possibly drain their faith and hope they had in powers beyond the surface of the world and restore some sanity to Witness's demonic mind.

In the distance, Witness's four friends followed. Like Witness-turned-into-Irina before, they were incorporeal and on this plane, they needed a body. When the camp put up tents for the evening, mortal faith lingered on, but in its dream form, the human being's faith weakened. Their emotions possessed cosmic significance, a power left unknown to them. She communed with these incorporeal spirits only at night. Witness could meet them in dreams. *Soon my friends. I am almost upon a place of darkness whereupon I can get you the bodies you deserve.* The incorporeal demons streamed past him in agitation like storm clouds cackling with streaks of lightning. They whirled about in desperate impatience ready to taste the misery of mortals in

225

the ways long denied to the dead. They craved life to consume the living.

In more ancient days, Witness saw secret caches of his own kind. There were sites, unknown nodes lurking just under the surface of the mortal world, where the plane of the Underdark entered through small pinpricks of necromantic energy. Several millennia changed the landscape, but Witness's spiritual being gravitated toward one. She directed the caravan there. By her estimates, they were as close as they were going to be before Irina Corovan stood challenged by another member of the caravan and the glamoured elves. Witness pulled the reigns to halt the horses, secured the coin purse, and folded out the steps of her wagon. "This is as good enough place as any to set up camp," she said to Mr. Grinsley. Mr. Grinsley, a roof thatcher, rode by her side like a lost puppy. He was almost always at arm's length from her. His balding face and gray beard betrayed a lust he felt for the enchanting Lady Corovan, which made him a useful oaf to Witness's purposes. He shouted to the others to set up camp, and the Lightdwellers stopped. Having spent the last three weeks on the road, which twisted into narrower improvised trails unkempt with forest growth, the travelers were exhausted, but did as Witness-turned-into-Irina commanded.

"I do not wish to be disturbed," Witness told Mr. Grinsley. "It is my time to pray in silence." Witness-turned-into-Irina went into the forest and did not return until nightfall.

Waiting till darkness, Witness-turned-into-Irina walked through the tented camps. Witness felt the dreaming dullness of faith and recognized the tent designs of four families. Witness sent out a psychic suggestion for the four women to awaken. They awoke in a trance under her power; Witness watched them closely since the second town outside Venda. Four young ladies ranging from seventeen to their mid-20s arose without flinching. They made little sound. Under Witness's power, they obeyed, and they trailed off into the warm night.

"What the?" Mr. Grinsley said as the stirring of motion awoke his laboring heart for Witness-turned-into-Irina who he saw off in the distance leading the women away. Nobody should be out this late, even if a noblewoman commanded it be so. There were many things in the nearby woods that could endanger all of them.

Some distance away, a gorge emptied into a ravine near a diseased oak, its branches withering in the lush ancestral forest. Witness pulled a branch, and a staircase led into the dark. "Enter," Witness ordered. Without hesitation, the four girls followed. Torches flickered and came to life as they entered. Mr. Grinsley eyed the doorway and the lever used to open the passageway. The secret chamber whispered to him.

Thick rooted branches carved up a small staircase that opened into a circular chamber. Four torches danced in the direction of the four winds. In this place, far away from the caravan, Witness's friends danced in spiritual form as low-hanging orbs of light. The air rippled as they encircled the young women. The incorporeal beings came through to the world of the living when the Prime Magus left the summoning circle in haste when he first called Witness forth. Witness orchestrated their arrival, coming here to this moment; the old space under rotted earth and tree in a place of life. Witness smelt the power and decay of death all wrapped into one in this ancient space. It felt good.

In his hands, Witness felt magick flow, powers granted to him in his very nature. Pink energy coiled around Witness-turned-into-Irina's hands like a snake. Mortal bodies looked up, the white of their eyes showing, awaiting the inhuman apparitions above. Their wills subdued; the mindless women stretched out their hands. In their minds, Witness felt only the bare whispers of struggle like the electricity in the air from a storm that passed miles ago. Witness-turned-into-Irina's spell connected them all, one will consuming the women until nothing remained.

Tucked away on the steps leading to the chamber, Mr. Grinsley watched secretly from the steps. If he moved, they would discover him, so he lay flat and as silent as possible. Fear and tears poured over him. Even though ignorant of the Hight Arts of magick, Mr. Grinsley knew death when he saw it. All mortals knew it when witnessing this power, or when witnessing the demon named *Witness*. This power caused the living to shiver, to recoil from it, or to find it mesmerizing. Coiling around Witness's arm the magick entered his chest and mouth. As Witness spoke, a vapor emitted from his mouth, the body of Irina Corovan now a conduit of power for the Underdark. The words of magick floated in the air with inhuman power. Like death, the words lurked there, a smell of rot redolent in the air. The air of death commanded Mr. Grinsley's innocence. Death enticed him to stay as the ancient powers held sway over his soul.

Witness arched his hands back and forth, the power surged. Above Witness-turned-into-Irina, the apparitions circled faster and faster now visible to the living. A white blur surrounded Witness and the four women. The air whistled and whooshed. Then, it fell silent, a deadly quiet. The fluctuating orbs entered and diffused through the bodies of the women. Fangs grew from their mortal frame, and the souls of the women screamed as they were evicted from their corporeal bodies. The white souls floated and found openings above. Mr. Grinsley swallowed hard as the women's souls exchanged places with the demonic souls that loomed above. Then, the swirling storm clouds joined the moment that the white souls receded into whirlpools of necromantic energy. Those openings into the Underdark collapsed, the dimension receding to the in-betweeness this place radiated. Fleshy membranes morphed from their back, and the flesh paled. Their living mortal glow vanished.

During the last scream, something snapped in Mr. Grinsley. He saw his breath turn cold, the vapor visible as he breathed despite the summer air and summer moon far above. Every bone in his body shifted to a state of panic. His body flooded with heavy breathing and adrenaline. *That's it. I'm out of here.* His foot found the stone step, and fell hard upon it. The sound echoed and alerted the powers of the Underdark. *One heartbeat.* With preternatural speed, Witness moved over to him, grabbing his hood and pulled hard on it with the enhanced strength unseen in centuries. His body went limp as he moved throughout the air like a rag doll. *Two heartbeats.* He was powerless, a body in motion hurled through the air. *Third heartbeat.* Mr. Grinsley hit the stone floor, and his leg snapped inside. Pain shot through him, and he screamed a glorious scream. His emotion and anguish were raw food for Witness. Witness-turned-into-Irina reveled in the psychic trauma, devouring those emotions like little chocolates.

Mr. Grinsley saw one woman, radiant blonde hair and innocent blues transformed into demonic black, fangs growing as she hissed in delight at the decadent scent of flesh. He turned his gaze. Frantic, he saw that he was in a circle, an ancient chalk or paint, that now glowed red with runes of ancient magickal script. A woman with fiery red hair smiled fangs. Her green eyes contrasted with the deadening stare of her otherworldly mouth. The third, a brunette, came from behind. She ran her elongated mortal claws over his ripped pant leg like a connoisseur caressing the ingredients of a fancy meal. The tender flesh seared from her touch. He drew his leg back in panic, curling into a ball as best he could despite shattered bone while the last woman, copper-hued flesh and dark hair stared at him like a predatory bird. She cocked her head to the side, her inhuman eyes staring straight ahead. "Can I have the first bite?" Bitter eyes and screeching shrills from the other three challenged her claim to drink from the man first.

Witness walked over to him. "Irina, I swear. I didn't see anything. Please. Let me go, please!" Mr. Grinsley begged.

"Oh" Witness-turned-into-Irina said softly. "My sisters haven't been corporeal for eight centuries. They're hungry." She put the boot of her heel on his chest. "Growing girls have to eat." The last things Mr. Grinsley saw were the flashes of red, the boiling sensation of his blood, and the repeated stabbing of teeth into his neck, arm, and legs.

****

For several hours, the morning sessions divided plans and responsibilities. Thayumeer ordered the Wyverns to rest, and the galleons circled the city. Repair crews set to work; minor mages transmuted the spell-raised walls of ironwood back from the smoldering ash of Allurian aggression.

Flight of the Ravenhawk

Sylvara was fatigued. Both her and Kal walked out of the gathering tree. Kal instinctively grazed her fingers with a light touch, and Sylvara hesitated. Unnerved, Kal walked a little ahead. King Thayumeer joined moments later. Behind them, elven lords left. Sylvara held back unsure of the touch of a human heart once more as Kal set off downhill into a section of the city.

When Kal left the Gathering Tree, the elves looked at him, some fearing and others smiling. Lowborn and highborn gave him wide berth. Looking determined, his eyes felt betrayed by Sylvara's reluctance to love, and a bitterness seeped in. He could not notice the reluctance and sense of dread that intertwined in the many expressions he received. Part of the problem was the power he displayed, the swallowing of the army and the sinking of three destroyers all in one day of battle. With the power of the node, creation gave him a powerful gift, but people confused that gift with *his power*. Whereas a necromancer stole that power from life for death, a Lightdweller employed those energies when given them by the Source. This gift, or power as most thought of it, was not Kal's but that of the Source and whatever power he had to give freely from his own lifeforce. He walked for what seemed several hours in and through the winding and twisting turns of tree tunnels, steps, and the shaped earth of elven architecture.

Before he knew it, Kal came upon the Lightdweller temple in the human quarter, a simple wooden A-frame attached to a dome of stone where people could gather before and after service. At the height of the roof, a stained-glass window of elven craftsmanship depicted the Star of Galadrana. In the back, Brother Whittaker oiled the wooden seats. Kalero walked into the framed space.

"Prince Kalero," the Abbot muttered. He did not come out, instead continuing to clean the benches. Lying down and stretching his short body, the old man turned his head while wiping the cloth on the underside of the seat. "What brings you out this way?" A long moment grew as Kal left it unanswered for some time. Smiling, Brother Whittaker carried on and waited for Kal to answer in his own time.

"I hurt a lot of people yesterday. Some of them my own countrymen, the very ones I would rule if I…" His voice trailed off, and Kalero folded his arms, vulnerable and afraid. Kalero looked out the doorway, shamed and not wanting to make eye contact with the priest.

"Now everyone is looking at me. I'm either savior or something to be feared."

Brother Whittaker sat up, and put down the rag and oil. "Listen, Kal. Can I call you that?"

He nodded *yes*. Brother Whittaker patted the seat next to him. Kal sat uncomfortably, the priest looking solemn. "We don't have much to go on, scripture wise. In fact, it can be read and re-read to get what you want out of it. The Source is this, the Source is that, even you, a scholar, have your own encounters with it, your own interpretations."

"What's that have to do with swallowing an army?" Kal asked. "I killed the very people yesterday I swore to serve."

"I'm starting from a different place, but I'll get to your concern in just a second," Brother Whittaker said. The priest held a book in his hand and shook it emphatically. "We can get a lot out of it, especially all the figurative language, symbolism, prophecy, and historical references. Some sections are prophecy, others history, other parts pure allegory, and still other parts sometimes all three."

"That's generally the best way of looking at it, I think," Kalero stated.

"Then, you're like scripture."

"Wait, what?"

"You're gonna have to accept that you'll be feared and loved, sometimes both. You must stop worrying about being all things to all people because people will make up their own minds about you and some will serve your brother. You can't expect your own self-conception to be theirs, so stop feeling guilty about what you can't control," Brother Whittaker explained. "In the end, you must do your duty. Be at one with something greater than yourself and heed its call."

Kalero chuckled. "Like scripture and be in balance with that which is."

"Like scripture," Brother Whittaker repeated tapping Kal on the head with one of the holy texts. Kal managed a slight curl of a smile, his spirit lifted. "The hurt will linger. Don't deny yourself that. You'll be living with that for a lifetime. There will always be more conflict, and probably more lives taken by both sword and magick as the days move forward. I'm glad that you feel remorse about it. I'm glad that you abhor violence against Allurians. That makes you different, but you must embrace your own Source-nature, too. Conflict can be minimized, but it's inevitable as others resist the will of the Source. Insofar as you serve the Source, the point *is* to always keep in mind its balance, and see yourself as restoring a bit of it to the world, even when you take the lives of others."

"Thanks," Kal said.

"Be true to yourself, kid by being true to the Source."

"Funny thing. I used to see the world as truth to be known, told about in the scrolls and books of the academy. But out here...I don't know what I am saying." Kal was lost in his own words, a confusion growing in the back of his mind. Muffled through the walls, children played in a nearby courtyard. The sun parted clouds. A cascade of blues, reds, greens, and violets beamed into the room before them.

"If I had a guess, you're talking about how strangely disanalogous an academic notion of truth is to practical lived-experience. It's different being out here amongst the people, living in a printer's house," Brother Whittaker said. "Or fighting alongside soldiers. Your birthright is a privilege and rank. There are expectations within that structure about how things ought to be, and sometimes we tend to think those structures are as natural as the laws of light in the science of optics." Brother Whittaker moved his hand through the stainglass rays of light to emphasize the point. The fact that you are mageborne, even if you hadn't been of

237

the Tremayne line, comes with its own privileges."

"The remorse at killing those who sided with Nash…"

"Is a response to a situation that defies the expectations of order. Allurians vie for power all the time, but the founding noble houses have never warred with each other openly. Your feelings are only natural, but they do not serve you or your people."

Kal laughed half-heartedly. "Sometimes, I'd rather be writing books than being out here." He looked down at folded hands. "Are you saying that my response will not help them in the long run?"

"Yes. Some social truths are formed in situations beyond our control, and we contribute to their reality and the force they have over us. Consider a deer path over yonder." Brother Whittaker gestured to the wall on the Southern edge. "Deer run a path over there. The elves find it. They walk on it. What happens to it?"

"The path erodes the grass and fauna," Kal said.

"And is the path sustained by everyone's acceptance of it? The path would certainly be overgrown if both elf, human, and deer stopped using it. All parties sustain the path, each contributing to the truth of the path by responding to it, constituting it, and it's just as easily destroyed if all three of them cease using it altogether," Brother Whittaker said.

Kal's eyes narrowed. "I must respond to the slain Allurians in a way that defies expectations. I must reject the old path."

Brother Whittaker raised his hand parallel to the ground, and shook it slightly. "Sorta. You have to realize that in rejecting one path, you also start opening up another."

A long silence grew between them and lingered for a moment.

Remorse dissipated. Pushing up out off the bench, Kal bowed to the priest, laughing, and hands folded in respect. Returning the gesture, the priest picked up the rag and oil once more and returneding to his chore as if Kal never bothered him.

Chapter 16

That night, Kal's dreams reflected not the anxiety and remorse of a previous day. Instead, the night became blissful before sleep, lulling Kal into a dream. Kal sat atop a mountain, the dream cast in a blue light. Sitting with legs crossed, he meditated on that mountaintop, an inner peace not shaking to a lurking groan just at the edge of mountains. A calm overtook him. *In breath 1, out breath 2...all the way to ten and back again to one.* For the moment, he had strength to keep calm, and it wasn't that this presence disturbed him initially. Something was coming, trying to push him off the mountain into a state of panic, yet his breath anchored him. His exhale became a radiant shield.

Crows started to land on his body. He saw himself there, perched like he was watching one's life as part of an audience rather an acting it out for himself. Crows flew ahead and above, swelling like ocean foam in stormy waves. The murder of crows obscured all light, and the roar became thunderous, indistinct, and muffled by crows. The crows called out to something far below the mountain. A river ran with black ichor, an odor that he could smell within the dream. Something pushed at the edges of those rivers. Something rose from underneath like the pressure of lava bubbling up into the fiery interior of the hollowed molten mountains. In his bed, Kalero awoke.

Immediately, he extended his perceptions to the area trying to encompass Zalanthas in one general spell of detection and insight in the early morning hours just before sunrise. *Relief, fear, and exhaustion*. These emotions were not his. These emotions came from the ancient wood carried on the back of the treesong. *Something came. Something festered in the powers beyond—above or below*. Kal could not tell. He never encountered this power, never knew its kind though the Ancestral Wood called out to him. The power was beyond his ken, even if he now possessed the secret of being a wizard of pure thought. Such power comes from without, by listening within, but youthful ignorance also limited his ability to know what this presence was.

Quickly, Kalero dressed and grabbed his satchel. Making haste, he skipped several stairs jumping only to the landing between floors of Dorn's residence. The landing thud woke

Rigela and Dorn, but Kal wasted no time to explain. Some power came, an unnerving power more primordial and ancient than the dragon-imbued armor of Darnashi. This magick was similar, something more diffuse than concentrated. Kalero never felt anything like it before, and his instincts and training moved him. He sprinted out the door on pure intuition of its presence. Commotion stirred beyond the wall as signal arrows whistled through the air. The guards still wrestled with the thought of near-invasion and massive loss of life and friends they knew for centuries just days ago. Shouts of the elven guard and horns blew, cutting the tension. When Kal reached the wall, the sentries never stopped him. In his haste, Kal quickened his pace, letting magick take over. He travelled as the sand through the air materializing on the tower overlooking the field and ridgeline where he had swallowed an enemy army. Where an army stood, refugees now gathered in fluid throngs. His staff-standard still remained planted firmly before the ridgeline.

Unlike the force of the army, caravans of a few thousand people swelled before the gates. Magickally disguised as humans, the two glamoured elves that manned part of the underground railroad came out of the group.

They were scouts, part of Anarkana's spy network. "We must speak with Lady Anarkana," the first shouted in elven. The second elf, appearing human, spoke more urgently. "We need healers, too. Lots of healers." When the sentry heard this, he looked at Kal.

Closing his eyes, Kal extended his hand, and reassured the sentry that looked back at them. "I cannot sense anything…though, I think, it's the pain. They've been through a lot." His vision faded, though he felt the unyielding sense that something was not right. That something not right could just be the collective suffering before him.

The sentry said nothing for the longest time overwhelmed by the scene before them. Then, the young elf told another over his subordinate over his shoulder, "Wake Lady Anarkana, and tell her of the news." And you," he pointed to the elven guard next to Kal, "Fetch the healers. Tell them they'll need lots of food and water. I estimate two thousand." He nodded and left Kal's side.

Before the healers arrived, Lady Anarkana came to the gate below. She never noticed Kal in the upper tower. Bitterness, resignation, and tactics—that's all he sensed personally in Lady Anarkana. Like a predator, she hid her intentions well. Kal hated her lack of transparency. He augmented his hearing, and turned away from them staring out to the humans and some lowborn elves camping out. *These people must be Allurians, Lightdwellers?*

Some bore wounds, scars and burns. Improvised bandages, and sticks for crutches decorated many who could no longer stand, but fell into the wet morning dew of ferns and grass. Several refugees wore the Star of Galadrana pendants, a common symbol of the Lightdwellers borrowed long ago by a unified faith splintered between elves, dwarves, and humans. Someday, Kal would talk to the ancient elven King; they would discuss how the Lightdweller faith had been in centuries past. He shifted his attention to the conversation below.

"Lady Anarkana," they bowed.

"Report," she commanded.

Neither agent identified themselves by name. Kal noticed they used the informal conjugations making the spies intimates of Anakana. The first spoke taking in long breaths. "We came through the latest route adjustment. These some two thousand are all that remain of the Allurian Lightdwellers."

"What?" she asked. This was the first time Kal ever saw outward emotion displayed on her stoic face. "The Allurian empire covers most of the known lands. Certainly, there are more Lightdwellers in this world than these refugees." It felt more like a statement than a question. Anarkana, too, fingered the Star of Galadrana in her right hand. She offered a silent prayer.

"We've gathered reports from the survivors. Following King Darnashi's declaration, the Lightdwellers are to be killed or driven from Allurian land, their temples and wealth forfeit to the crown. Some of the temples were destroyed by the advancing skyfleet, others by fearful towns," the first explained. Like a blow to the stomach, Kal bit his lip and held back tears on the tower. This was his brother's doing. A rage filled his heart.

"And the clergy?" Lady Anarkana asked.

"In every instance, he or she is the first to go," the first said.

The second scout shook his head. "That's not all ma'lady. In the Forests of Turiel, a curse hit our caravan. At first, we thought it flu, but it's something else. The forest seems to eat the human kin, but never preys on us. We can't explain it. People just go missing, and we find only the briefest measure that someone was there. Glasses, small bracelets on the ground, a spattering of bone dust, but never is the ground disturbed. Whatever this danger is, it cannot be tracked, and possibly comes from above." Anarkana seemed impatient with this news. If it were any other time during her long life, Anarkana might dismiss such stories as products of the overly-superstitious lowborn, but not today. Too much had happened already.

"I know you've been through a lot. I must ask the both of you one more thing. Move the very sick and wounded inside the walls. Admit no one that can be treated outside. Use your best judgment, but minimize the exposure of Zalanthas until we know more of your curse."

Kalero descended into the tower. He decided to wear a glamour, an illusion. Whatever power was here, it might be here for him. He put on the seeming of a healer, his wizardly arts more advanced than an average village healer, but not as advanced as the herbal and forest-based druidism of the elves. He doubled as a healer in a pinch, but the healer disguise would put him out in the open. The danger no longer mattered. He should find whatever this danger was, and exterminate it.

****

In the camp, the compulsion of the Prime Magus's binding was strong now. Witness felt the loss of her will gradually more and more. She pulled out a mirror and spoke the spidery language of magick. The Prime Magus's face appeared.

"I am close now."

"Good."

"Master, it's become harder to control myself. Your binding is too great. If I see him, I will attack, yet I am not to use my powers and reveal myself. I can sense him coming, walking into the camp as surely as he senses me now. If I am to remain useful, I need the freedom of my will to plan a better attack."

Back in Venda, the Prime Magus reclined in the blood-stained satin chair. The Prime Magus rubbed his beard pensively. "You have three days of freedom. Find an opportunity, or I'll send you back to the pit from whence you came." She grimaced and felt the immense power of the human's will. It was strong. On the back of her wrist, a small three burned its way into her skin.

"I'll report back when the deed is done."

He left his chambers to return to the King.

The Prime Magus entered the throne room. King Darnashi weaved his armor-encrusted hand as if a dance, the gauntlet's black joints looking like falling dominoes in the intricacy of Darnashi's hand movement. Chained on every limb and suspended in air between granite pillars, General Litner floated on glowing pink energy chains. His stomach tore open and re-knitted over and over again with the gentle hand movements of Darnashi's spellcasting. The man bit off his own tongue in screaming and merely gurgled.

"My agent is in Zalanthas, just outside the wall."

"Good," Darnashi smiled. "That will give us another chance to get rid of my brother." The words were sad, somewhat distant from his viciousness. Darnashi's face twitched, his mannerism reluctant at causing General Litner anymore suffering. The Prime Magus had better act quickly while nobody was here.

"There, there," the Prime Magus embraced him. "Don't be scared." Under his breath, the small pink vapor of rot and magick entered King Darnashi's eyes. The Prime Magus renewed the spell of influence and control. Fury and hatred returned to those eyes like the unveiled moon returning its glow to night. The sadness all but disappeared. King Darnashi felt the eye take over what the Prime Magus wanted him to see. With a wave of his hand, the Prime

Magus smiled and locked the door. As Litner's body hit the floor, a large clunk reverberated in the throne room. Litner laid on his stomach, weak and alive. The chamber windows morphed into dead steel and closed out the light, and the torch flickering sounded like banners in the wind.

Closing his eyes, the Prime Magus sensed the wards he wove all around this room, even from prying eyes of the Wizardrium itself. He sat in the throne, impatiently gesturing to King Darnashi. "Let me see what you were doing before I disturbed you." Darnashi repeated the motion. Once again, pink magical chains formed atop of pillars and stretched General Litner's body before them. He shook his head as tears fell on his cheeks.

The Prime Magus sipped Darnashi's wine. "Good." He sat forward and put his hand out. Try rotating your wrist when you speak this incantation, and add the following circle with the finger. "This is how you part flesh from bone. Now, you try." The Prime Magus gestured the goblet toward General Litner.

"Yes," Darnashi replied. His eyes were lost in a fogged sea.

General Litner saw the glowing eye and the pink haze of the Prime Magus's control. King

Darnashi obeyed him perfectly. It was the last thing he saw in this world before his flesh split from bone entirely.

Flight of the Ravenhawk

About the Author

J. Edward Hackett, Ph.D. is an academic philosopher at Savannah State University who rather than engage in metaphysical speculation in process metaphysics is off building magick systems in his world of Apeiron. Fantasy fiction is itself an exploration of concepts in extreme for him. In fantasy this exploration is limited only by the imagination in much the same way that philosopher employs the intellectual imagination to solve problems that science, common sense, religion, or art cannot solve on their own.

In his debut novel, *Flight of the Ravenhawk,* Apeiron is a world as boundless as its origin coming from Anaximander's fragments. Wizard nobles vie for power in the Allurian Empire. Airships shoot lightning cannons. Elven archers fly atop griffins, and a dwarven kingdom is buried deep in the mountains far from elven or human spires. At the same time, Ed's fiction cannot help but be inspired and instantiated by concepts that come from ancient, modern, and 19th and 20th century philosophical systems of thought. It's in his blood.

Ed grew up scattered across the Midwest and Mid-Atlantic states. Born in Lakewood, NJ and spending most of his life north of Pittsburgh, PA, Ed has been traveling to other worlds since he bought the Star Wars D6 RPG book by West End Games and Mage: the Ascension from White Wolf as a teenager. He grew up on Magic the Gathering, 80s fantasy movies, and many comics of the 90s amidst the rust belt of Western Pennsylvania.

Although a professor, Ed still goes to imaginary worlds with his friends at the age of 39. He's in a classic AD&D game. His philosophizing meshes with the sensitivity to imaginary worlds. Just recently, he contributed an article about environmental ethics and the animated movie Wall-E in the upcoming *Disney and Philosophy.* He's edited another pop culture and philosophy volume called *House of Cards and Philosophy,* co-edited an academic volume on phenomenology entitled *Phenomenology for the 21st Century.* He also published his first solo academic book called *Persons and Values in Pragmatic Phenomenology* (2018). When asked if she was a philosopher once, the great Simone De Beauvoir said, "No, I'm a writer." Upon hearing that many years ago, Ed has tried to write for many audiences and emulate her example.

Ed has been married to his wife, Ashley, since July 30th 2006. They live in Savannah, a magickal place in its own right and before that they lived in Cleveland. They have two cats: Olive and Lulu. Ed absorbs the sunlight of the beach, practices zazen, and while writing and teaching philosophy and other courses in the humanities, he shoots landscape photography. Despite all of this, his greatest joy is teaching and writing. "Writing fiction is simply being philosophical with narratives rather than directly talking   about   concepts."

Don't forget to connect with J. Edward Hackett on social media! You can find him on Facebook, Twitter, Instagram, and on his blog, *The Horizon and the Fringe*.